Other Works By B. Heather Mantler

The King's Ransom

Committed to Her Enemy

For Wealth and Glory

B. Heather Mantler

Mantler Publishing Prince George

ISBN:0986875961
ISBN-13:
Library and Archives Canada Cataloguing in Publication

Mantler, B. Heather, 1987-   For wealth and glory /
B. Heather Mantler.

ISBN 978-0-9868759-6-0

I. Title.

PS8626.A676F67 2012   C813'.6   C2012-
901984-4

For all those people who gave me feedback on my first book. I appreciated it and hope this one will not have the same problems.

PROSTER IS BORED AND DECIDES TO ATTACK BATEND

Prince Proster of Grankle finished the meat off the drumstick in his hand before throwing the bone to the dogs in the corner. The dogs went after it in a frenzy. Some of Proster's men sitting nearby them laughed at the dogs' behaviour.

"I am not certain which is worse," Herwin said, "the dogs or the men."

"The dogs should be fed more often," Proster said not even glancing in that direction, "The men are drunk out of boredom."

"Has your father allowed you to get more food for the animals?" Herwin asked.

"He claims that there was a drought last year," Proster answered, "As such there is no extra food to give to the animals."

"Yet he fills his plate to brimming and throws the leftovers away," Herwin said.

"He believes me too far removed from him to know that there was no drought and that he just does not wish to feed my animals," Proster said, "But when I speak with the people working the land, they said that the crops were plentiful and that if I had not been off fighting that war for my father I would have enjoyed it. Unfortunately, my father is using my absence as an excuse not to provide me with the supplies that I need."

"Perhaps another kingdom needs warriors," Herwin said.

"My father is at peace with everyone," Proster said, "and Alaric has declared that he wishes to raise his children in peace, if I am to take the men back into battle I have to start the war myself."

"It would hardly be the first time," Herwin said, "There are several kingdoms who can be provoked into a war. All you need is a map and a plausible reason."

"When I defeat whatever force that is sent to attack me," Proster said, "I crawl back here and ask my father for any scraps that he feels his seventh son is worth. The warriors have gotten bored with these battles. They can face any force without fear.

"My father is too distracted with Alaric and his sons to bother with any of the rest of his children. I am tired of sitting around here waiting for a bone to be thrown my way, or to hope that he finds some use for me. I am tired of it all!" Proster slammed his fist into the arm rest of his chair. Herwin did not even twitch. No one else in the room even looked in their direction to see what Proster was upset about. If they needed to know Proster would make a big announcement.

"I live in a kingdom that has no use for me and I am supposed to like it," Proster said as he got up to pace, "Do you know what my father told me when I went to see him yesterday?"

"No, I do not," Herwin answered.

"He told me that I had brought a lasting peace to the kingdom," Proster was no longer just pacing, but each time the stomp of his foot hit the floor was loud, as if he hoped that the dissipated energy would remove the anger, "He said that I should become a priest like he always wanted me to be. Priests he would need, warriors were useless to him. Do you know what I told him?"

"No, I do not," Herwin answered.

"I told him that Saint Ingram hardly needed any more priests," Proster said, "There were already so many spreading the good news about him. He said that such talk was blasphemy against the gods, whichever ones he meant. He changes the god he worships more frequently than I bathe. The fact that there are many saints, but only one god seems to have slipped passed him completely."

"Or perhaps he just simply does not want to believe in one god," Herwin said, "He has always wanted to keep his options open."

"And he will go to hell for that," Proster replied, "I just do not want to sit around waiting for him to do it. I beginning to think that there should be a limit on the number of children that a king should have. After the third one, the king and queen can only have another if one of them dies. That would prevent nine children and williness to feed only three."

"So, what do you suggest we do?" Herwin asked, "Since battle is the best way to gain food to feed us as well as the animals. It also keeps us from getting so bored that we find starving dogs to be funny."

"We start a war," Proster answered, "but we do not bother fighting just one battle before coming back here. We fight to conquer. We fight the war, gain the ground and keep the spoils. That should provide the challenge we need as well as food for us and the animals."

"Your father will want his share," Herwin said.

"Very true," Proster replied, "but if we start the war and fight until we have our own space and resources the only way he will get anything from those resources would be to attack us for them. It is either find our own place or become thieves in his cellar."

"Unless I am mistaken, we already are thieves in his cellar," Herwin said, "I doubt he would give up the wine barrel willingly."

"I sent Garrick out with some men to find food and drink," Proster said, "He had money with him. If he chose to steal over buying, I know nothing about it. Besides, it beats letting them loose on the town."

"On that I will agree," Herwin said.

Proster sat back down in his chair.

"How are we going to start a war?" Herwin asked, "Most of the neighbouring kingdoms have a treaty with your father because of us."

"There is no treaty with Batend," Proster said.

"That is because no one wants a treaty with Batend," Herwin said, "According to all the stories coming out of that kingdom, the king has practically run the place into the ground. People are leaving that kingdom in large numbers. Most of the neighbouring kingdoms do not even trade with Batend. The only industries there are mining and forestry. The only reason they have farm land is because they cannot get wheat from anyone else without there being high tariffs on it. I would not be surprised if the king was ruling about three people by the end of five years."

"There will be more than three people in the kingdom at the end of five years," Proster said, "a former diplomat for the country told me that his prisons are full. If he ever needs workers he can just out the prisoners to work. His army would not leave him, so he will always have men. The army is the one thing he is willing to fund. In fact, his army is better funded than any other on the continent. That is part of the challenge. If we can defeat his army then we deserve to rule his kingdom."

"There are some other things that stand in the way of that challenge," Herwin said, "and I am not talking about what your father would say or do if word of this reached him. King Thedious is known for having informers and we are a rather loose lipped group."

"If my father wants to stop us from going to war with Batend then he needs to provide us with the wages and supplies," Proster said, "He has shown no interest in doing that."

"Or we could all get honest jobs," Herwin said, "that is still a possibility."

"Yes, I hear the farmers near here are in need of some extra hands," Proster said, "Shall I offer them your services?"

"Not until your father punishes us for the failure of a war we started," Herwin said, "that is if we have not died in battle."

"If we die in battle then any such requests are useless," Proster said, "We are most likely to be dumped in a grave to stop us from creating a stench. And I would not expect there to be separate graves."

"Once dead, none of us will care," Herwin said, "When are we going to attack Batend?"

"First we have to get close to the border," Proster answered, "Then we have to create an incident that will give us a reason to attack. We are going to have to do this in an underhanded way if we are going to succeed."

"If we create an incident, your father might try to negotiate peace to prevent a full scale war," Herwin said.

"He has policy of not negotiating with Batend," Proster said, "No one does. So far any such incidents are dealt with on the local level or ignored. My father does not want to go to war, but would not be bothered if someone eliminated the problem of Batend. Except maybe if his son started the incident and did it all on purpose."

"And what excuse do we have for getting closer to the border?" Herwin asked.

"Mati's father would be willing to put us up for a while," Proster answered, "And since he would provide food for our animals then it is a far better place to be than here where we cannot get food for us let alone our animals."

"That sounds realistic," Herwin said, "What answer would I get if I asked Mati?"

"Confirmation of what I just said," Proster answered, "Especially after I have had a chance to talk to him."

"When are we leaving?" Herwin asked.

"Two days from now," Proster answered, "If we do not leave soon we are likely to lose many of our animals. I will tell the men tomorrow morning at practice."

"Very well," Herwin said, "if I may be excused there is a lady I wish to say good bye to." Herwin stood up.

"You have a day," Proster said.

"A day is but a moment when spent with this lady," Herwin said.

"You do not have to ask my permission to go," Proster said, "It is not like we are in court or at council."

"Perhaps it is just the difference in our stations that has me ask anyway," Herwin said, "Despite everything you do to erase it, you are still a prince and I am still the son of a whore. And you will always be a prince."

"Go see your lady," Proster said, "She obviously does not mind you being the son of a whore."

"Not at all," Herwin smiled before walking away.

Proster looked over the rest of the room. His warriors were still busy drinking all the wine from the barrels that Garrick had stolen from the royal cellar. Many were drunk and the rest were getting there. Mati was not there, but Proster remembered him leaving much earlier. Proster knew that Mati had a whore he regularly visited at the nearby brothel and that was where Proster was most likely to find Mati. Proster did not know what else to do so he left the hall. His warriors were not likely to do much more than drink themselves into unconsciousness and he had seen that more than enough times.

Proster left the building. The night was warm with the late summer breeze blowing passed and bringing the scent of freshly harvested wheat. There were only a few buildings with lights on. Most of the village that surrounded King Thedious's summer castle was fairly small and most people did not stay up late. Proster figured that his father gave him the use of the guard's hall to keep his warriors contained. He also figured that his father did not know about the brothel when he let Proster and his warriors come to the summer village.

Proster started down the road. There was no one else out and moving. Proster went passed all the shops and entered an alley way. At the end of the alley way was a door. Proster knocked on the door. Less than a minute later the door opened, to reveal a lady dressed up in a scarlet outfit that showed more skin than was proper.

"Prince Proster," the lady tilted her head to one side and leaned on the door as if she was assuming that he was here for her. She smiled at him and Proster could see the gold tooth that was near the back.

"What can I do for you?" the lady asked in a low voice that suggested she already had a couple of ideas.

"I am looking for Mati," Proster said.

"I'm more fun than he is," the lady said.

"But talking to you does not get me what I need from him," Proster said.

"He paid for the night with Lilybelle," the lady said as she fluttered her lashes at Proster, "It didn't sound like they wanted to be disturbed."

"Madam Chari, I have no interest in what you are offering," Proster said, "I am however, interested in talking to Mati. You can disturb him or I can discuss your business with my father. Right now he is into his grandchildren, which means he wishes to clean anything that might be considered dirty. Several brothels in the capital have already had to close their doors and their members were forced find labouring jobs. Would you like to be next?"

"I'll go get Mati," the lady's voice went cold as she straightened up, "Stay there." She closed the door. Proster stood for a minute before leaning against the wall to wait.

A minute passed before the door opened again. Mati stepped outside wearing only his pants. He looked like he had been asleep.

"Yes?" Mati asked.

"I am going to talk to my father first thing in the morning," Proster answered, "I am going to tell him that your father invited us to visit him. That arrangement is better than the current one since your father is willing to feed us and our animals."

"If King Thedious asks I will tell him that my father invited us to go stay with him," Mati said, "Is there any other information I should know if asked?"

"We will be leaving in two days," Proster answered.

"Fine," Mati said, "Anything else?"

"No, that is everything," Proster answered.

"Then I will see you in the hall tomorrow for your announcement," Mati said.

"Good night," Proster said. Mati went back inside the brothel. Proster turned and went back down the alley way. Proster stood at the entrance to the alley way for several minutes. He did not want to go back to the hall yet, but there were very few other places to go at this time of night. Sounds came from down the street causing Proster to step back into the shadows of the alley way. Two of his father's guards came down the street. They were leaning against each other and talking in loud voices as they tried to tell each other to be quiet. As they got closer Proster could smell the drink on them and moved to stand with his back to the stone wall that was behind him. The two men lurched into the alley way and went passed Proster without noticing him. They knocked on the door at the end. The door opened and the men went inside. The door closed behind them. Proster continued to stand there for several minutes as if waiting for anyone else to show up in the alley way.

Finally Proster started in the direction opposite to the hall. He walked down the road, passed all the houses and out of the village. Here were fields of wheat separated by the road. There were a few trees edging along the road, but otherwise there were none in sight. All the forests in the area had been chopped down for farm land. This was the case in all of Grackle. People would rather have farm land than forest. Proster thought this was a foolish thing, because trees had so many uses while they were still in the ground. The only time he had told someone that they had laughed at him. The man had claimed that there were more uses for a tree once it has been cut down than there was if the tree was still standing. Proster had asked what would serve those uses for the wood once there were no more trees in Grackle. The man just made a throw away gesture and said that they would import it. Proster thought that was good news for countries that had lots of wood to sell. After all they could break Grackle paying for wood that they could still have if they managed their forests correctly.

Proster continued along this country road until he came to an hill. He went up to the top of the hill and stopped there. In front of him he could see that the farm land went on until it stopped at a group of buildings that marked the next village. Proster turned around and saw practically the same scene, though it was a slightly shorter distance to the buildings. There was also the summer castle of his father's. King Thedious, Thedious's wife, Alaric, Alaric's wife, and Alaric's three children were all staying there. If it was not for the servants they needed it would be a very empty place. All the rest of Proster's siblings had stayed in the capitol, some with their husbands or wives and some with their occupations. That was the one thing King Thedious was good at was getting his children to realize that they would not be dependant on him for the rest of their lives. That was why King Thedious wanted Proster to become a priest where he would be fed, clothed and not looking to his father for money, or handouts as King Thedious called them. Proster called them. Proster called them payments for waging wars in his father's name.

Proster sighed as he sat down in the middle of the road. He wanted very little from his life. A good fight, good friends, and money to keep doing both. Perhaps someday he would find himself a bride. Unfortunately, Proster had met all the noble women of Grackle and every time he spent time with any of them he found himself repelled by them. He stayed away from the brothels his men frequented for much the same reason. At times he wished it were different, after all with that kind of problem you cannot marry and produce an heir if you cannot find a wife that suits you. But more of the time he found the lack of interest in women beneficial. If he was not interested he was not distracted by them.

Proster was happy that his brother, Alaric, had a wife and children. The kingdom had heirs and the royal line would not be in trouble. It also meant that he was unlikely to see the throne. Aside from his father's recent venture into peace, Proster had no interest in ruling Grackle. His father and brother could deal with that headache. But what was the point in attacking Batend? Proster asked himself. Was it just to see how far he could get before being defeated? Was it to see if the king would change if attacked? Was it because the army of Batend was rumoured to be unbeatable? Or was Proster in it to become king of Batend? And if he did defeat the current king of Batend would he take over the position? He did not really want to do all the work just to hand the whole kingdom over to his father. That would only put him back in the exact same position he was in now.

Perhaps being king of Batend would not be too bad. He would rule much differently than his father did. He would be able to control his own destiny. Why should he settle for anything less than king of Batend? It was not like the current king did a very good job of ruling the place.

Proster smiled to himself as he set that goal in the proper place in his mind. He was going to be king of Batend or die trying. Proster got to his feet and headed back down the hill toward the village he had come from. The depression had lifted now that he had a goal in mind. Even the lack of trees did not bother him as he walked passed the farm land.

Light was starting to appear in the sky as Proster reached the village. As the first rays of sunlight came over the horizon Proster could hear the people starting to move in their houses. Based on the lack of clouds it was going to be a good day to start harvesting the wheat.

Proster was thinking more of heading to bed, but he knew he had things to do first. He knew that his men were either passed out drunk or still drinking, if there was any wine left. Proster went to the summer castle. Since it was the changing of the guard, there were no guards at the gates so Proster walked in without having to stop. The servants were just starting to get to their duties. King Thedious was not likely to be up for several more hours unless someone woke him. Proster went through the hallways to the great hall. This was where King Thedious held court when necessary and also where the family ate. It was about the same size as the hall for the guards, but it had much better quality of furniture. And of course, King Thedious's banners were on the wall of the great hall. Proster did not bother putting up the banner that had been made for him when he was born. It was too much trouble and his warriors were more likely to treat him as one of them if the fact that he was a prince was not rubbed in their faces all the time.

The great hall was empty this time of day. The servants would have cleaned it before they went to bed and none of the royal household would be ready for breakfast. Proster braced both doors open before going inside. Then he went and sat down at his father's place at the table. He sat there and waited.

It was less than ten minutes later when the steward entered the great hall. He entered expecting to see it empty and just in need of the doors being closed.

"Oren," Proster called out. The steward looked over at Proster and immediately stopped reaching for the doors.

"Prince Proster," Oren the steward bowed and then straightened up, "What may I do for you today?"

"Breakfast would be a great start," Proster answered, "Supper last night ended up being a little light."

"Anything else, Prince Proster?" Oren the steward asked.

"Yes, I need to speak with my father," Proster answered.

"He is still asleep," Oren the steward said.

"Well, after you bring me some breakfast you can wake him," Proster replied.

"Very well," Oren the steward bowed again and then left the great hall. Proster smiled to himself.

King Thedious groaned at the light coming through the window. Charmaine had not bothered to close the curtains after she stood at them and sulked for an hour last night and now the sun was streaming in as if it had nothing better to do.

"Your highness," Oren the steward's voice came from the doorway.

"Close the curtains," King Thedious ordered, "And let me sleep."

"I would, your highness," Oren the steward said, "But Prince Proster is in the great hall demanding breakfast and to speak with you."

"I already told him we do not have any food to spare," King Thedious said, "What does he want?"

"He did not tell me anything else," Oren the steward answered, "But he looks like he will stay there until you speak with him."

"Then he can sit there and wait until I get up," King Thedious said and rolled over so that the sun was out of his eyes.

"Charmaine is awake and heading down the stairs for breakfast," Oren the steward said.

"What!" King Thedious sat up in bed.

"Charmaine is heading down the stairs to have breakfast," Oren the steward repeated. He appeared undisturbed by King Thedious's reaction. King Thedious climbed out of bed and grabbed the pants that had been left on the chair. He started tugging the wrong leg on.

"Serve them breakfast," King Thedious ordered, "Do whatever you have to do prevent them from being alone together."

"Yes, your highness," Oren the steward said, "I will also send Eldon to help you get dressed." Oren took one step back out of the room before closing the door.

Proster was sitting there sharpening his knife when his father's wife came into the great hall. He ignored her presence as he continued to sharpen his knife. Charmaine saw him and her eyes lit up. Her walk slowed as her hips moved more when she walked.

"Good morning, Proster," Charmaine's voice was low and silky.

"Is my father awake yet?" Proster asked. He put the boredom into his voice in hopes that Charmaine would not try what she usually did.

"How would I know?" Charmaine said, "We do not sleep together, we have not done so in such a long time I do not even remember if he snores, it leaves a woman in need of a real man." Charmaine kept coming towards Proster as if she did not notice his response to her.

"I am sure that Oren will wake him," Proster said, "then it should not be too long before he comes down."

"I doubt Oren would do that," Charmaine said, "Oren has orders not to wake Thedious unless it is an emergency." Charmaine sat down on the arm rest of the chair Proster was sitting in. She smiled down at him. He did not bother to look up at her.

"Breakfast is served," Oren the steward announced in a booming voice. He was carrying a tray with two plates on it. Charmaine sighed as she stood up. She moved to the next chair as Oren the steward came over to the table. He placed a plate in front of each of them. Proster put his knife away before picking up the chunk of bread that was on the plate.

"Is there anything else I can get for you?" Oren the steward asked. He was still standing at the table as if he was ready to do whatever Proster ordered.

"Has my father been woken up?" Proster asked.

"I send Eldon up less than a moment ago," Oren the steward answered.

"Then that is all," Proster said. Oren the steward did not move immediately.

"I am sure you have *other things* to do at the moment," Charmaine's voice was cold.

"Of course," Oren the steward said. He turned to head for the door. Charmaine watched him or a moment as if she suspected that he would not actually leave. When he seemed to be she turned to smile at Proster again.

As soon as Oren the steward left the room, two maids arrived. One had a dusting cloth and the other had a broom. When she saw them, Charmaine scowled at them. The maids started their jobs close to the door.

"Breakfast is not the appropriate time to be sweeping and dusting," Charmaine called to the maids.

"We are sorry," the maid with the broom said turning toward Charmaine, "But this is the only time we have to get this done."

"They can stay," Proster said.

"Thank you, Prince Proster," the maid curtsied before turning back to her sweeping.

"But I would prefer if you did not sweep or dust while I am eating," Proster said, "Why do you both not take a seat at the table? Perhaps you can tell us how you ended up working here."

"If you prefer, Prince Proster," the maid with the broom said. She leaned the broom against the wall and the other set her dusting cloth down. Both came to the table and took seats farther down the table. Charmaine looked angry, but she did not say anything. The maid that had been sweeping was the taller of the two. She had brown hair and hazel eyes. The second maid had more curves than the first. Her blonde hair was in twin braids that came over her shoulders and her blue eyes was clear as if it was possible to stare straight into her soul. Proster was sure that Charmaine had noticed this as well as he had and she was also comparing their ages to her own. The maids were probably sixteen, where Proster knew that Charmaine was thirty years of age. The brown haired one had a certain quality that Proster liked, but he felt no strong attraction to any of them.

"Let's start with your names," Proster said.

"I'm Jacinda," the brown haired one said, "And this is Maida."

"We were hired by Oren," Maida said, "This provides for our families."

"Should you both not being getting ready for marriage?" Proster asked.

"I am engaged," Jacinda said, "The wedding is to be next summer."

"My father is arranging a marriage for me," Maida answered, "But it is all by letters and is taking some time."

"I see," Proster said.

King Thedious entered the great hall. The maids slipped off the chairs and curtsied low as he walked passed.

"Why is it that you demand my attention?" King Thedious demanded of Proster. He had noticed the maids and waved them away. They quickly left the room.

"I wanted to tell you that tomorrow me and my warriors will be leaving," Proster answered.

"Already?" Charmaine pouted, "But you just arrived."

"Where are you going to go?" King Thedious asked.

"Lord Sika has invited us to stay with him for a while," Proster answered, "and he is less likely to let my animals starve to death."

"All of this could have waited until later," King Thedious said.

"After this I intend to sleep most of the day and spend the night preparing to leave," Proster replied, "there was no other time that I had to tell you."

"Well, you have told me," King Thedious said, "Anything else you feel the need to tell me?"

"Your wife is a whore," Proster said as he got to his feet, "perhaps you should find her a chaperone."

"That is none of your business," King Thedious said.

"Now it is not," Proster said before leaving the great hall. Proster barely got the doors closed before he could hear his father and Charmaine starting to scream at each other.

The maids were outside in the hallway.

"Now we cannot get out stuff," Maida said, "we'll have to ask Ona for some more supplies." Maida started down the hallway. Proster's eyes were on Jacinda. She started to follow Maida when Proster touched her shoulder. She turned back to him.

"Does you betrothed mind sharing?" Proster asked.

"Not that I am aware," Jacinda answered with a smile. Proster took her hand and she followed him out of the summer castle.

The maid was gone when Proster woke up. The afternoon sun coming in the window bothered him more than her leaving him. After all she had work that she had missed and had to catch up on. Proster got out of bed and washed before getting dressed. He left the room. There was no one waiting to speak to him outside, but he could hear some movement from down in the hall. Proster went down there. He found most of the men awake and shuffling quietly at the tables. The barrels of wine were now full of water and men were taking mugfuls out of it in order to sooth the headaches. Some of the men looked over at him when he entered, but no one bothered to do anything. Proster went over to the table where Garrick was seated. Garrick had the accounts book in front of him and looked to be deep in thought.

"Something wrong?" Proster asked.

"Yes," Garrick answered looking up at him, "If we stay here and wait for you father to feed us than we shall all be dead in six months, because we will be broke in one and the animals will not last very long in their present state and that is with stealing more than we are buying. King Thedious not properly paying us for that last couple fights has really set us back."

"Herwin around?" Proster asked.

"No, I believe he will be with his lady friend until tomorrow morning," Garrick answered, "Do you need him for something?"

"No," Proster answered, "I was just wondering if he told you about our discussion."

"What is the plan this time?" Garrick asked.

"We are headed for Lord Sika's place tomorrow morning," Proster answered, "From there we will create an incident that lets us attack Batend without it looking like we caused a war to start."

"To what end?" Garrick asked, "The supplies to start the war will break us and no one is going to pay us at the end of that fight."

"At the end of that fight we will either be in control of all Batend or we will be dead," Proster said, "I do not plan on needing money after I am dead."

"Who gets Batend when we are finished?" Garrick asked, "Right now no one is going to buy it off of us."

"We are not going to sell it," Proster answered, "and if my father wants he can battle us for it."

"You are not talking one small battle," Garrick said, "You are talking taking on an army that is very loyal to their king and rumoured to be unbeatable."

"Of course I am," Proster said, "because I am beginning to see the horrors that will result in us staying here. Why not die fighting for something?"

"I am with you," Garrick said, "When are you going to make the announcement?"

"At supper," Proster answered.

"I will take some men and see if I can find a meal fitting for such a celebration," Garrick said.

"Not so much wine for this meal," Proster said.

"As you wish," Garrick said. He closed the accounts book and took it with him when he got up.

Out of a hundred warriors there were only ninety-seven at supper, but Proster did not mind. The other three knew what was going on and were preparing for the trip. Most of the meal had been eaten when Proster stood up at his place. The volume quieted, but not enough. Proster climbed up on the table with his glass in hand. All the warriors fell silent and turned to him with their own glasses raised.

"On this day, I raise my glass to each one of you proud warriors," Proster said, "Each of us became a warrior for reasons other than there it is merely being a necessary job. We became warriors for the glory of battles won. We became warriors for the wealth gained in those battles. We became warriors to beat down our enemies. We became warriors to be lifted up in victory. None of us sit here in this hall because we want to face defeat, unless it is the defeat of our opponents in battle.

"I fear that staying in this village we will face starvation and poverty at the hands of my father, King Thedious. He has become complacent. He wishes not to go to battle. He claims the goal of peace. He says that peace is only possible through peaceful means. He tells me that warriors are a dying breed. He informs me that we should go find ourselves proper jobs so that we may fit into his new idea of what a kingdom is.

"I have brought you all here to say that my father has turned into a very foolish man. If he believes that there is no longer a need for warriors then we shall leave his presence. We will find other places to seek glory and wealth. We will be an army with a leader, but no king. We will decide what battles to fight. We will create our own destiny, our own fate.

"So, today I raise my glass to celebrate our next adventure together, our next battle together. Tomorrow we will set off to find our own place in this world, where my father's new policy of peace does not cause us to starve. Drink with me. To Wealth and Glory."

"To wealth and glory," the warriors replied in unison. Then everyone drank. Proster got down off the table. Proster set his cup on the table before leaving the hall. The warriors would talk among themselves, but they would follow him anywhere. He headed to his room to start packing.

Proster looked over his warriors. They were packed and waiting in a group for him to say it was time to leave. Each one had his own bags as well as the animal he was assigned and a few had extra items that they had charge of. Proster had his own pack and that was all. He got arguments if he tried to take more and he argued with anyone that suggested he should not carry his own pack.

"Everyone is ready," Herwin told Proster, "What are we waiting for?"

"The sun," Proster answered, "If we leave before the first rays of light then no one is likely to see us leave and I want my father to know we are gone. The sun should be up soon."

"All right," Herwin said. He went back to double check his own pack. Proster looked at the hall of the guards his father had let him use. The stone building would last a long time, but it was likely to fall into disuse after they left. That was part of the reason Proster had demanded that they clean everything properly. It also made sure that no one forgot anything.

There was light in the sky. Proster turned back to his men. All their attention was now on him.

"This is the day we leave behind this village," Proster said, "and this is the day we leave behind this king. Today we go to where we will find our next fight, our next battle. We will gain more from this than we will ever lose. But today we march."

As the sun peaked over the horizon Proster got down and started marching along the road. His warriors fell in behind him in semi formation. They were not guards and did not form perfect squadrons, but they march along in rows of three men across. They were not in step with each other, but they moved much faster than any squadron of guards and no one was left behind.

A few people came out to watch when they heard the warriors march passed. Proster did not acknowledge any of the people, though some did wave to the group. There were no tears and life of the residents would go back to normal with the warriors gone. The only one that might be sorry to see the warriors leave was Madam Chari and Proster was sure that she would get over it.

Oren the steward was standing at the gate of the summer castle. He stood there as a witness to them leaving, but gave no sign of anything else. Proster continued without giving any acknowledgement. He had already told his father he was leaving, if his father had not believed him that was not Proster's problem.

By the time the sun was above the horizon, Proster and his warriors had left the village behind. The roads were packed dirt, the sky was clear, and the sun was hot. It was a beautiful day for a walk, but a tiring day for a march. Proster stopped his warriors every time there was a place that they could get water. He also stopped for a few minutes in places where there was shade. The warriors did not complain about the marching, but they seemed to appreciate the breaks. It slowed down their progress and by nightfall they were only three quarters of the way there. When the night fell, Proster had his warriors stop for half an hour. Some slept, some sat and ate what they had, and some just rested. Proster spent the half hour sitting on the grass with his back to a tree and listening to Garrick and Herwin argue about the best way to create an international incident. There were plenty of ideas, but most of them needed some work. Proster absorbed the ideas and let his mind mull over them.

At the end of half an hour Proster had his men continue on their march. With the loss of sunlight there was a loss of heat, though it was not cold. It felt like weather that was made for marching and made the going much easier. They made good time and got to the estate of Lord Sika before midnight.

Lord Sika father was not awake, but his steward was still up. He directed them to a hall for guard near the front edge of the estate. The warriors filled the hall with themselves and their supplies. Proster was given the captain's room. It was cramped with merely a bed and a trunk for his belongings. The warriors were quiet, but they still made noise. That did not stop him from collapsing into the bed and going to sleep.

The bright light of the afternoon came into through the shuttered window and on to the bed. The light was reflected off the sheets and into Proster's face. Proster rolled over to get away from the light and smacked himself into the wall that was next to the bed was pushed against. Proster sat up and rubbed his ear. He looked around, but there was nothing around to see. There was still noise coming from outside the room. Proster got out of bed and changed his shirt before leaving the room. Most of his warriors were awake and doing things, but there were a few still sleeping.

"Mati and Herwin are looking for you," Garrick said from where he was sitting on a chair beside the door, "They are at the manor waiting for you. I am told that there is food there as well."

"Nothing has happened here?" Proster asked.

"Sleeping, waking up and eating," Garrick answered, "Lord Sika is very generous as far as food goes. He even sent food for our animals."

"Then I will go to the manor and talk with him," Proster said, "After that there needs to be a discussion about creating an incident."

"I will be here," Garrick replied.

Proster left the hall. He headed across the grand estate to the manor. The acres of estate left the summer castle and even the castle at the capital looking poor. Every plant looked like it was placed where it was growing. The garden beds were beautiful colours. There were several areas with just trees. The paths were carefully laid cobblestones. The manor itself looked like a farm house compared to the grounds. There appeared to be only three storeys and had a flat front. There were several large windows on the ground floor. The stairs going up to the front door were made of marble. When Proster reached the door it opened before he could stop to knock. A servant stood there holding the door knob with one hand and bowing to Proster. Proster stepped into the manor. The servant closed the door behind him. Before Proster could turn and ask where he should be going a man dressed as a butler entered the entry way through a door on the right.

"Prince Proster?" the man asked.

"Yes," Proster answered.

"Lord Sika is waiting for you in the study," the man said, "This way." The man turned and went to the doorway to Proster's left. Proster followed him. The doorway led to a short hallway with a door off each side and one at the end. The man went to the one at the end. He opened the door and stepped inside. The man stepped out of the way of Proster.

"Prince Proster," the man announced as Proster stepped into the room.

The study must have taken up the whole corner of the first floor of the manor. There was a fireplace that took up one wall. Aside from the large window and the door, all the walls were covered in shelves and the shelves were full of books. Closer to the window than being in the centre of the room was a large wood desk. Sitting behind it was a man with white hair and a long white beard, but a young face. Despite the wealth that surrounded him the man had not an ounce of fat on him. There were five comfortable looking chairs in front of the desk. Mati was sitting in one and Herwin was sitting in another. They all looked over at the announcement.

"Thank you, Jevon," the man behind the desk said as he stood up, "Welcome Prince Proster. Please come in and have a seat."

"Thank you," Proster said. He sat down in one of the empty chairs. The door closed behind Jevon as he left the room.

"You and your men are welcome here," Lord Sika said, "but from the sound of things you will not be here very long."

"We only plan on being here long enough to put our plan into motion," Proster said, "While we are here, I greatly appreciate your generosity."

"It is nothing," Lord Sika said, "What is this plan?"

"Starting a war with Batend," Proster answered.

"Their army is reported to be undefeatable," Lord Sika said.

"It is better than staying in this country and starving at the hands of my father," Proster replied, "I do not wish to have to beg for scrapes from people or depend on generosity. I want to be able to provide for my warriors. My father has made treaties with all his neighbours except Batend. That makes Batend the best target. I am sure that my warriors can come out successful against any army that Batend can produce."

"Very well," Lord Sika said, "Where are you going to start?"

"With sending spies over to scope out the situation there," Proster answered, "although any information you and your people can tell me would be most helpful."

"I do not have much information to give you besides the order from King Thedious bans trade with Batend," Lord Sika said, "however, I have a couple men in my employment that cross the border and trade with occupants of the nearest town. I can send them over to speak with you this afternoon."

"That would be appreciated," Proster said.

"The only problem you might have is that they know about King Thedious's order not to trade with our neighbours over the border and maybe suspicious of you asking about their activities over there," Lord Sika said, "It may take a little bit of persuasion to get them to provide you with the information they have,"

"Thank you for the warning," Proster said, "I will take that in consideration when I speak with them,"

"Is there anything else you will need?" Lord Sika asked.

"Not at the moment," Proster answered, "I have not talked to my advisors yet and as such I do not have a plan of attack. However, if we ask you for something that you do not feel comfortable say so and we will find another way to obtain it."

"Your father might be my king, but I have very little loyalty to him," Lord Sika said, "And he has done little to inspire loyalty from me. I will do what I can to help you and I will not send him any messages about what you are doing."

"You will send one message to him about what we are doing," Proster said, "You will send a message that we have started a war, but you will wait until his response will come too late to stop us."

"Certainly," Lord Sika said, "That I can do, but you will have to tell me when that time is."

"I will," Proster said, "In the meantime, I need to borrow Herwin so that we can discuss our plan."

"Of course," Lord Sika said, "I do not want to prevent you from doing anything."

Proster stood up and so did Herwin.

"We will speak with you soon," Proster said.

"I will send my men around," Lord Sika said.

"Thank you," Proster said. Then he left the study followed by Herwin. They did not say anything as they walked back down the hallway and through the doorway to the entrance way. The servant at the door opened it for them. They stepped outside before the door was closed behind them. Proster went down the marble stairs with Herwin beside him. At the bottom Proster looked around before continuing along the path. He did not see any servants around.

"What did you get out of your conversation with Lord Sika?" Proster asked Herwin.

"He has created everything within the walls," Herwin answered, "He cares nothing for any king and does not want any king to disturb what he has created. He will help us because his son is loyal to you. If it was not for Mati he would have denied us entrance to his estate. Mati is his only son and Mati's mother died when he was young. His father never remarried and lacks interest in ever doing so. That makes him a good ally, but we need to be careful. He is not against King Thedious as long as King Thedious does not bother him."

"We will keep our visit as short as possible," Proster said, "But we do not have any ideas as to what is on the other side of the invisible line between here and Batend. So short might be a month or two."

"I can take a squad and scout out the town," Herwin said, "And with the men that Lord Sika said had information we should be able to figure out what is happening in Batend."

"We need to know what happens at night and during the day," Proster said, "We will start scouting tonight and continue for the next two weeks. We will use the information we can get from his men and then we will get as much of our own as possible. Hopefully, within a week we will have a plan of attack."

"I am ready," Herwin said.

"We will see," Proster said, "After all Batend's army is supposed to be invincible."

"Do you think that will stop us?" Herwin asked.

"That has never stopped us before," Proster answered, "Why should it this time?"

Herwin smiled as they continued along the path.

SCOUTING BATEND AND THE FIRST BATTLE AGAINST THE FORCES OF BATEND

The room that was meant to be the captain of the guard's sleeping quarters was crowded with Proster sitting on the bed, Herwin sitting on the trunk, Garrick leaning on the wall beside the window, and the three men standing just inside the door. The three men were about the same width and height of Proster's warriors. Proster guessed them to be in need of strength in their jobs as traders for Lord Sika, and not for just loading and unloading the goods from the wagon. They all had brown hair and brown eyes with solid looking jaws. Proster guessed them to be brothers. The middle had a beard, but otherwise they looked very similar.

Proster and Herwin had come back here and talked to Garrick for a while about the plan to attack Batend before the men that Lord Sika talked about arrived. Proster had told them to come in without thinking about how full the room had been with just him, Herwin and Garrick. Now the room was crowded with six men inside it. The men had not shut the door behind them for which Proster was glad. It had taken Proster a very short time to convince the men that he was not going tell King Thedious anything about their activities. Perhaps it had been that Proster had been dealing with this sorts of men all his life and had never been much on reporting them to anyone in a position of authority.

"Tell me what you know of the town that is just over the Batend border from here," Proster said once they were finished establishing some trust.

"It is a small town," the middle man said, "There is a guard station. There are between seven and ten guards there at a time. The nearest city is a day's ride from it. The town is surrounded by ranches and farms. Most of the residents do not care what you do as long as it does not interrupt their lives. The king of Batend has not yet made that town the focus of his reorganizational efforts, but there are signs that it is coming. The people that live in town are worried about it, but right now it does not affect their lives.

"Town is set up in a square and has a wall built around it. There are guard stations on each end of town. There are two ways in and out of the town. There are two guards at each entrance at all times and well as some that wander the town at regular intervals. There is one main street, which is where the businesses are. The houses are scattered is a disorganized layout that start at the back of the buildings that make up the main street."

"History tells of soldiers building the town to protect the border," the man to the left said, "It was built so that it was difficult to take over."

"But it is also difficult to defend once the attackers are inside the walls," the middle one said, "if it would help you, we can take three of your men the next time we go across."

"That would be most helpful," Proster said.

"Considering the amount that we are delivering and picking up we need the help," the middle one said, "We will give them at least half an hour to look around town before bringing them back."

"Okay," Proster said, "When is your next trip there?"

"Two days from now," the middle man answered.

"I will have some men ready to go with you when stop here on your way," Proster said.

The middle man nodded and the three turned to leave.

"I have one more request," Proster said.

The three men turned back to him.

"Is there a map of the town that I could study?" Proster asked.

"There should be one," the man on the right answered, "I think I know where it is. I will send it to you."

"Thank you," Proster said. The man on the right nodded and the three men turned to leave. This time they left the room without any interruptions.

"Do you still want scouts to go out tonight?" Garrick asked once the men were gone.

"Yes," Proster answered, "It sounds like the town has more defenses than I thought it would. That means we will not be attacking straight on. So we need to know every way into and out of that town as well as anything we can about the guards. Herwin will take his team out tonight as we talked about."

"Okay," Garrick said.

"I will gather the men I need and explain what we are doing," Herwin said as he stood up.

"Good," Proster said. Herwin left the room.

"Is there anything else that you need?" Garrick asked.

"No," Proster answered, "Do not let me take up any more of your time."

"You are my commander," Garrick said, "I have no time of my own, it is all yours to do what you see fit with it."

"Out!" Proster commanded, "Go use up my time somewhere else."

Garrick saluted as he tried to keep the grin off his face. Then he left the room. Proster rolled his eyes before taking out his pack. He took out his armour a piece at a time. He set it out on the bed until it resembled a metal skeleton. The pieces he used regularly were showing signs of wear, but the pieces he never bothered with were a shiny as the day he received them.

Proster strapped on the pieces of armour he used for training. He also strapped on his sword. Then he left the room. Some warriors that were in the hall were sitting, talking and eating. Proster went outside to the field that was next to the hall for guards. There was an exercise field. There were many warriors already out there, practicing. Proster joined them.

Proster finished fighting Lance and Redmond and had moved to the sidelines to watch the next bout. Someone touched his arm. Proster looked around. At first he didn't see anyone, then he saw the boy standing beside him.

"What do you need?" Proster asked.

"My father told me to bring this to you," the boy answered holding up a scroll case.

"Thank you," Proster said taking the scroll case from the boy.

"Do you mind if I watch for a while, sir?" the boy asked gesturing toward the fighters.

"I do not mind," Proster answered, "Just keep out of people's way."

"I will," the boy said. The boy went over and sat down on a bench near the practice field. Proster went back to watching the match.

When Proster was finished training for the day he took he took the scroll case back to the captain's room. In the scroll case was one piece of parchment rolled up. Proster unrolled it on the top of the trunk. It was a map of the town that the men promised to send over. Proster studied it for half an hour before taking with him when he went to find Herwin.

A week of scouting passed. Herwin took men to the town at night and the men that traded with the town took some men and introduced them to residents of the town. So far the reports that had come back to Proster was that there were only two ways into or out of the wall that went around the town, climbing the wall would be difficult, and that the guards were not townspeople that were recruited to be guards, but men send from the capital on orders of the king. The townspeople and the guards got along as long as they did not disturb each other's work. There had been a few clashes between the two groups, but mostly it was the guards trying to carry out the king's orders that the residents resented. The traders did business with the residents, but did not socialize with them so Proster's men did not get a chance to talk with any of the residents. Overall Proster was certain that the town would not be difficult to conquer. The difficult part was going to get the rest of the army to show up to fight them.

Proster, Herwin and Garrick met and discussed issues relating to a plan of attack. They went over all the information that had been collected up to that point. They discussed what they need to know before they could launch a successful attack. Then they discussed a plan of attack. When they finally finished their discussion Herwin and Garrick went off to where they were sleeping.

Proster put on his traveling cloak and left the captain's room. Most of the warriors had gone back to sleeping at night and training during the day. Mati was the only who went anywhere other than the hall and the practice field, but Proster had instructed his warriors to stay where they would be available at a moments notice. The warriors seemed to think this had to do with the impending battle, not that Proster wanted to avoid trouble with Lord Sika.

Proster tiptoed through the hall and avoided waking anyone. He nodded to the guard at the door on his way out. The guard nodded back, but did not say anything or block his way. Proster went out into the night. On the edge of the practice field was one group of warriors that sitting around. They had not readjusted their sleeping schedules and Herwin had been using that for his scouting runs.

The group looked up at Proster as he came towards them and the conversation was halted.

"I need three men to come with me," Proster said.

"Another scouting run?" Ordway asked.

"Not exactly," Proster answered, "But it does involve the town."

"I will come," Ordway said as he got to his feet. Two other men also got to their feet. They came over to where Proster was standing and the rest of the group went back to their conversation.

Proster took the lead as they left Lord Sika's estate. The guards at the front gate did not even see the four men as they slipped away.

It took a couple hours to walk the distance to the border and across to the town. By then the town was silent and dark. The only lights were at the entrances on either side of the wall. These were lanterns hung out to alert them of anyone coming.

Proster and his men stopped before they reached the light.

"Which building is the one the guards sleep in?" Proster asked Ordway.

"That one," Ordway pointed to the one on the left, "We usually go in the other side. The guard on the other side is awake, but there is only one."

"We want the left one this time," Proster said.

"Why?" Ordway asked.

"Because if we just outright attack Batend we get in trouble for it," Proster answered, "It there is a reason for our attack then we do not get into as much trouble."

"So what are we doing here?" Ordway asked.

"Stealing guard's uniforms," Proster answered.

"Okay," Ordway said.

The group started for the entrance to the left. The guard's residence was built into the wall so that there was door that went straight into it and the gate beside went into the town. The four men stayed close to the wall. Proster tried the door. It opened without a problem and there was no shout of alarm from inside. Proster signalled for Ordway to come with him and the other two to stay where they were. All three nodded with understanding. Proster entered the guard's residence and looked around. It was a small room. There was an empty chair beside the door and a pile of weapons beside a door that was on the other side of the room. Proster moved forward as quietly as he could. Ordway entered the room behind him. Proster went across the room to the other door. He opened it a little bit and looked inside. There were six bunks each with a bed on top and bottom making enough room for twelve men to sleep. In the centre of the room was a table with twelve chairs. There were six men sleeping in the beds. All were sound asleep and had not heard Proster and Ordway moving around. Proster noticed that all the men were wearing uniforms as if they could be ready at any moment for duty and worried that his plan would not work for a minute. Then he saw a laundry pile close to the door he was peering out of. Proster slowly opened the door and stepped into the room. None of the guards moved. Proster went over to the pile of uniforms and gathered them up. He handed them to Ordway, who was standing in the doorway. Ordway took them as Proster went back into the room. He gathered the guard's helmets before he went back to the door. None of the guard's moved. Proster went back into the smaller room and closed the door behind him. Then he and Ordway left the guard's residence. They closed the door behind them. The four men headed away from town.

Once they were at the edge of the last farmer's field they stopped. It was not much further to cross the border to the farm on the other side. The four of them stopped to put on the guard's uniforms. All four uniforms were a little tight in the shoulders and chest, but the warriors could wear them. Proster had to roll up the pant legs on his. They hid their clothes under a bush.

"We are going to do property damage, steal some things and let the uniforms be seen by the people," Proster told the three men, "But avoid hurting the people."

"Yes sir," the men replied.

Then the four of them headed for the farm.

The farm was a small one. There was a farm house, a barn and a scattering of other buildings. The four men went through every building except the farm house. There was very little worth stealing in most of the buildings. The barn held straw from last year and two work horses.

Proster took the work horses out of the barn. Despite the noise they were making, the farmer had not woken up. Ordway and one of the men went to knock down the outhouse while Proster and the other man went to the barn. Proster and the man each lit a lantern then waited. When they heard the crash of the outhouse hitting the ground Proster and the man threw the lanterns into the old straw that was in the barn. They left the barn and grabbed the reins of the horses. All four men went a distance away from the barn. They stopped to watch as the flames started to get bigger. The flames were eating the straw and were starting to lick the walls of the barn. It would not take long before the whole thing was burning.

A minute passed before the door to the farm house opened. The farmer stepped outside and stared at the barn. He saw Proster and his men. He did not move as he watched them. When none of the men moved the farmer went back into the farm house. Proster guessed that it was to protect his family.

Proster and his men took the horses and walked away from the farm. They had done what they had come to do. They had done some damage and the farmer had seen the uniforms. It was a good start to Proster's plan. Tomorrow he would see if there was going to be any more night time trips across the border.

They went across the border to where they had hidden their clothes under a bush. They took their clothes out and changed back into them. Then they headed back to the town with the uniforms and the horses. At the town Proster and Ordway returned the uniforms while the other two men put the horses into the stable that the guards used for their horses. Then the four of them headed back to Lord Sika's estate.

Proster's eyes opened and he sat up before his brain registered that he was awake. The bright sunlight did wake him up a little more. He blinked at the brightness and looked around. He was in the captain's room and everything was as it had been when he went to sleep. There did not seem to be any reason for him to wake up. The sun was at its height in the sky so it was noon and earlier than he would usually wake up.

Then the knock came again at the door. Proster rubbed the sleep out of his eyes before getting off the bed. He changed his shirt. Only then did he open the door. Mati and his father were standing there. Herwin was standing a little ways to one side.

"Yes?" Proster asked.

"I was wondering if I could have a word with you," Lord Sika said.

"Certainly," Proster replied opening the door wide enough for Mati's father to enter the room. Mati and Herwin stayed where they were in the hallway. Proster closed the door behind Lord Sika. Lord Sika sat down on the trunk and Proster sat down on the bed.

"What is it?" Proster asked.

"For several months now there have been people from Batend coming across the border to steal things from the people that live near the border," Lord Sika answered, "This has been a problem, but no one has ever seen the thieves. The claim from the guards on the other side of the border was that the thieves were from this side and we just could not identify them. However, farmers on the other side of the border never have any problems with theses thieves."

"You believe the thieves are from that side but you cannot prove it," Proster said.

"Exactly," Lord Sika said, "But last night the thieves struck again and burned down one of the barns on our side. But the farmer saw them before they took off."

"So, who are they?" Proster asked.

"The guards from that side of the border," Lord Sika answered, "The very men that we have been dealing with in hopes that the thieves will be arrested. I am tired of this and so are the people around here. I was hoping that you and your men could do me a favour that goes along with your plans to battle Batend."

"You want me to confront the guards with the information," Proster said.

"Or just attack the town for the destruction they had caused," Lord Sika replied, "Something that will make this stop.

"I will have to discuss this with my men," Proster said, "We were not planning on attacking until the end of this week."

"What else do you need to know?" Lord Sika asked, "I will see if I can get you the information."

"It is not so much information as some planning that needs to be done," Proster answered.

"I do everything I can to protect my people," Lord Sika said, "And I have been unsuccessfully in one area only and that is these thieves. I want them dead and lying in the gutter. It you can do that I would be most grateful."

"I will discuss with my advisors and we will send word of our decision with Mati," Proster said.

"Thank you," Lord Sika said. Lord Sika stood up and left the room. He did not close the door behind him. Once he was gone Herwin and Garrick were visible through the opening. Proster gestured them to enter the room.

"What did Lord Sika say?" Herwin asked.

"He asked that we take out the thieves that have been crossing the border to steal," Proster said, "Apparently we were not the first with that idea, but the ones that have been doing it have not been trying to start a war between the two countries. With this latest theift, Lord Sika is begging us to move up our attack to as soon as possible."

"Then when do you want to attack?" Garrick asked.

"I would say that it is best if we moved out tomorrow," Proster answered, "Then we can attack the town and get Lord Sika can send the letter to my father and we can get this war going."

"Do you want to announce this to the men or shall I?" Herwin asked.

"I will announce it at supper tonight," Proster answered, "It seems to go better if I announce these things."

"That is true," Herwin said.

"Herwin, tell Mati to let his father know that we are going to be leaving soon," Proster said, "But give it half an hour. I do not want Lord Sika thinking that we had planned for this to happen."

"I will," Herwin said.

"Anything else?" Garrick asked.

"Not right now," Proster answered. Herwin and Garrick nodded. Then they left. Garrick closed the door behind him. Proster laid down on the bed. He smiled to himself before closing his eyes.

Proster finished his meal with his men surrounding him in the hall for the guards. They were sitting at the tables that were set up for them. The food had been delivered and the men had been eating for a while. Proster had made sure that all his men were here. Lord Sika had already been informed about the plan to leave the next day. Proster took another sip from his goblet as he thought about the announcement he was about to make. It would please his men, many of whom were only happy when they were in battle.

Proster pushed his chair back to stand up. The men did not stop talking at first because they were not bothered if he chose to leave the table early. Proster stepped up on to the table. The room fell silent as all the attention turned to Proster. Proster held his cup in his hand and looked over the assembled men.

"We have spent time under my father's thumb and we have wasted a week sitting around here waiting for the right moment," Proster said, "Now the right moment has come upon us. We will battle with the army of Batend for control of that country. The Batend army is supposed to be undefeatable, but we have never been defeated in battle. I know that we can face anything and come out as the victors. I know that we can take on the Batend army and end up with control over the whole country. Tomorrow we will march into battle. Tomorrow we will start the war. Tomorrow's battle will not be a large one, or against many. It will be the foot hold battle against only a few and it will bring the rest of the army to the field on which we will have the larger battle. I expect you all to be ready to move and I expect you to tolerate the small battle because the large one will be glorious. In the end we will have our own kingdom with which we will do as we please. Then life will be what we make of it."

The men cheered. Proster raised his goblet. His men did the same.

"To war," the hundred men said in unison. Then everyone drank. Proster drank the rest of the wine in his goblet before surveying the group again. Then he stepped back down off the table. He sat down in his chair. The men went back to talking and eating, but there was a new sense of hope in the room. The men would be ready to move tomorrow as planned.

Proster sat there among his men yet apart from them. Despite the fact that he would never see the throne of

Grackle in his life, he was still Prince Proster. That made people, even his own men, hesitate to socialize with him. The stigma was an accepted fact of life to members of the royal family. Proster always felt that was wrong. The royal family should be open to having people of the kingdom come and talk to them. He had succeeded to a point with his men. They were willing to bring him their problems and question his orders, but socializing was still too far a leap for them. The only two men Proster counted as friends were Herwin and Garrick, his advisors, but even they did not seek him out for social interaction. They were far more likely to spend time with the other men for that. Proster guessed that people figured power to be very good at providing company, because otherwise they would look and see that the man in charge was alone up there on that pedestal.

Proster shook off his thoughts. He put his goblet on the table before standing up. Proster left the hall for guards. All the men were in the hall for guards so the practice field was empty. Proster walked over to the bench that the boy had sat on the other day. He sat down on it and looked around. Lord Sika kept his grounds in a state of perfectionism. Already the practice field had been tidied after the use of Proster's men. The servants must have done it after the meal was delivered. It seemed pointless to do such a thing to Proster, but he knew that his men would come back out after the mean and the servants obviously assumed that they were done with the practice field.

Proster went over the battle plan in his head. He did not expect battles to go exactly as planned, but he hoped that this one would. The men that were part of the first wave and the main part of the battle knew their roles. That would help things go closer to plan. The only thing that could foil the whole thing now was if the guards of the town reacted in irrational ways. Proster hoped that would not be the case.

An hour before dawn Proster was up, packed and watching his men get ready. He had already sent off the twenty men ofthe first wave. Lord Sika's servants had left provisions before they cleaned up of the practice field last night. Some of the men had eaten these for breakfast and some were putting them away for later. Proster gave no orders either way. There was no other breakfast and there was merely the dried food they already had for lunch.

The men were fairly quick to pack up their things, but that was mostly because they had not unpacked much. However when there are eighty men getting ready, not matter how organized they are, it still takes time. Finally most of them were packed and headed outside. Proster stayed and waited until everyone had left the hall for the guards. Since Garrick was with the twenty, it fell to Proster to make sure that there was no mess or belongings left behind. All the men had left and Proster did a walk around the room. There was no belongings left and the mess was very minimal. Proster headed outside. The men were lined up in what resembled a marching formation. Proster headed for the front of the line.

Once at the front of the line Proster turned to his men.

"We march," Proster yelled. Then he turned around and started to march. Foot falls started behind him as the men started to march as well.

Proster`s mind filled with the plan as his feet moved forward. *Herwin would take his nine men and head toward the guard`s residence while Garrick would take his nine men and head toward the guard post at the other entrance to town. Herwin would storm the residence with his men. There would be two guards in the outer room. They would take up arms and defend against the invaders. Herwin and his men would have a little trouble, but not a lot due to the poor shape the guards were in. The guards had not had to face a serious enemy in a very long time. They did not bother to keep in shape nor did they have much training beyond the basics provided to them when they joined the army. But the noise would be heard in the next room, where there would one other guard. If he was smart he would go out the door that led to town and realize they could go out the gate and get away. If he was foolish he would open the door to the smaller room and engage the attackers. Herwin and his men would take this guard out as well. Once all the guards were dealt with Herwin and his men would go into the town and start gathering the residents in the main square.*

Garrick and his men would come up to the two guards at the other entrance. The guards would defend their posts despite being outnumbered. They would fall, but the noise would bring the guard that was currently doing rounds in town, if he had not run off already. He would come either attack or realize that he could not defeat all ten men by himself and give up. Garrick would put him in the main square with the rest of the residents, but would leave an opening for him to escape. If he escaped, Garrick would let Herwin know and everything would go as planned. If he did not escape, Proster would send him to the next town with the word that Proster was starting a war. Once the residents were rounded up, then Herwin and Garrick would wait for Proster and the rest to show up. It was against orders to loot the town and there was not much else to do beside set up camp.

It was noon by the time Proster and his men crossed the border between Grackle and Batend. The farms started to show up. Proster had his men march along the road way and avoid marching on the fields. An hour or so after noon the town came into sight on the horizon. Proster stopped his men and gave them a break for lunch. He did not want his men too tired when they reached the town. He ate lunch as well.

Less than an hour later Proster and his men were back on the road marching towards the town.

As they got closer Proster could not see much for damage to the town, which he considered a good thing, but it was also hard to tell if the plan had worked. They were within shouting distance of the town when Ordway came out of the closest entrance to town and waved at them. He continued out until he met with Proster.

"We are ready to set camp around the town," Ordway said falling in step beside Proster, "Nine of the ten guards are dead. The tenth one got away before we could get him."

"Okay," Proster said before turning to the eighty men marching behind him, "Set camp around the wall of the city." Proster could hear the order being passed down the line.

"We have rounded up all the townspeople and they are in the main square," Ordway said, "Garrick and Herwin are there as well. We avoided doing damage where we could. There is one house in need of repairs as well as the guard's building at the other entrance."

"I will be headed into the town in a few minutes," Proster said.

"Yes sir," Ordway said. He headed back into the town. Proster stayed to observe his men as they started setting up camp. Once all the men had spots they were setting up Proster decided that it was time to go into the town.

He went through the closest entrance and passed two of his men. Herwin and Garrick were standing near the door that went to the guard's residence. Proster went over to them.

"How did it go?" Proster asked.

"Quite well," Garrick answered.

"The townspeople are gathered in the main square," Herwin said, "They are waiting to find out what their fate will be."

"I will go talk to them then," Proster said, "perhaps by the time I am finished they will be on our side of this war."

"And if it does not work out that well?" Herwin asked.

"We move camp tomorrow," Proster answered, "I do not intend to massacre a town just because they do not like how we work."

Herwin nodded. Proster headed for the main square with Herwin and Garrick following him.

All the townspeople were gathered in the main square. Women were holding their children and men were keeping their families close. None of them had been hurt, but all the eyes showed fear. They were farmers and ranchers, not fighters.

Proster stepped up on the platform that was set up. All the attention was on him. The people were waiting to find out what he was going to do with them.

When Proster had gone through the guard's residence for the uniforms he had seen the poster that the guards had put up. He could see several more put up around the town. The poster telling the townspeople that they were to send their harvest straight to the king and that the king would send guards to pick it up. And if people did not give up their harvest they would be punished severely. From what Proster had heard that poster was just the beginning of the king's new demands.

"Good citizens," Proster said, "I am sorry that we chose your town to gain our foothold into Batend. I have no wish to harm you or your livelihood. Nor do I have the wish to interrupt it. My goal is to defeat your king. That fight is between my men and his. However, we will be here in your town for at least the next two days, perhaps longer. My men and I will spend the time camped outside the walls of this town. My men have orders not to harm any of you and after this they will not interrupt your work. Once again I am sorry for inconveniencing you." Proster signalled his men before stepping off the platform.

Proster started toward the town entrance and his men followed him. They left town with the townspeople still standing in the main square. Once outside the wall the men went to help set up camp.

"Well?" Herwin asked.

"Now we wait," Proster answered, "By this evening we will know how long they will let us stay."

Herwin nodded before both of them went to help with setting up the camp.

The camp was set up and the men were busy with small tasks such as checking armour and sharpening weapons. Proster sat near his tent watching the world around him. He saw a man come out of the town's walls. The man hesitated a minute as he looked around. He looked like he was ready to bolt back inside if someone so much as turned towards him, but Proster's men continued with what they were doing. The man came out farther and still no one stopped him. Finally he headed out to the fields. Proster watched him start working in a field. The man was still nervous, but went on with his work.

A few minutes later several more men came out. They looked about as nervous as the first, but when no one paid attention to them they too went out to their fields. No more people came out of the town even though there were several fields empty. Proster was sure that more would come out over the next several days.

It was getting close to evening when the farmers went back passed Proster's men and back into the town. They were still very nervous, but did not quite look like they would jump out of their skin if someone said boo. Once they were back in town, Proster sent Garrick to buy some supplies for his men's supper. Garrick came out a short time later with what was necessary and passed it out to the men.

Proster was eating what Garrick had given him when a man came out of the town. The man was slightly better dressed than the farmers Proster had seen. He was also pudgier and older than the farmers. His brown hair was neatly combed to one side and he had the twitch of a politician sent out to negotiate a treaty between warring factions. Proster sat and watched him. The man looked around, trying not to move too much in case it brought attention to himself. Finally he spotted Proster. Then he came over to where Proster was sitting.

"I am Algernon," the man said, "I am the mayor of this town."

"I am Prince Proster of Grackle," Proster said, "Have a seat." Proster indicted the spot across from him. The man looked at the spot for a couple seconds as if considering whether it would be rude if he chose not to sit in the dirt. Then he seemed to realize what Proster had just said and sat down in the dirt across from Proster. He was speedy about it as if he moved fast enough Proster would not have noticed his hesitation.

"I have been asked by the townspeople to talk to you," Algernon said, "I would not disturb you, but they seem to think it is necessary. Of course, I did not realize that you were a prince of Grackle. That changes things considerably."

"What concerns the townspeople?" Proster interrupted before Algernon could get too far into being as humble and agreeable as he thought was best.

"They are worried about you and your men camped out here," Algernon answered, "They want to be able to work the fields, especially since it is getting close to harvest."

"My men and I will not stop them from working in the fields," Proster said, "We are just going to camp here until we get word that the army is headed this way."

"The king has an undefeatable army," Algernon said, "I am sure that you know that of course, but I do not think you completely understand, in fact most people do not. Several people have tried taking over Batend, but the king always beats them back, that is how come he is still on the throne. There have been attempts at takeovers and uprisings from the people and his own advisors trying to kill him and, and, and, well, all those things and more. The king is still there and has fought off all of it. There is nothing that can stop him. They claim that you cannot physically injure him. And then his army is one of the largest on the continent. The rumours are that his army is not made up of humans."

Algernon was just getting started into all the rumours he had ever heard about the king of Batend and his army. Proster let him talk even though he had heard the majority of it before. Algernon seemed to need the horrors to be told, especially if he was telling them. Proster decided that Algernon was in the position of mayor because he had inherited it not because he had been picked from the people. In Proster's experience most people did not pick a pessimistic person to lead them. It was just too depressing.

"I have heard all the rumours," Proster finally cut off Algernon, "I am prepared to face the army anyway."

"If that is your plan," Algernon said, "Though I am not sure how you plan to get the army to come to you. We are hardly important enough the occupying our town would cause the king any trouble. And your men killed all the guards."

"Those things are not going to stop my plan," Proster said, "The army will come to me and my men will defeat it. And until the time comes for that battle we will be camped out here."

Algernon nodded with a look of disbelief on his face. He was still trying to figure out how Proster was going to bring the army to a town so far from the capital it was a dot on a map without a name.

"You may go," Proster said. Still deep in puzzlement, Algernon got to his feet. He bowed before heading back into the town walls. Proster smiled to himself.

Herwin came over a few minutes later.

"What did he have to say?" Herwin asked.

"That the townspeople are worried about their lives and jobs," Proster answered, "Also that according to rumour, taking on Batend's army is suicide."

"I thought it was just merely invincible," Herwin said.

"The mayor of this town is not opposed to using hyperbole when it comes to describing our odds against the army," Proster replied.

"Did you tell him what our plan is?" Herwin asked.

"The army will magically come to us and we will fight," Proster answered, "He seemed very confused at the idea, but that is okay."

"Magically appear?" Herwin asked.

"The mayor claims that all the guards were killed," Proster answered.

"No, the last one was seen running from here fast enough that it is possible that people missed him,"

Herwin said, "The men followed orders and let him get away."

"But the mayor does not know that and he does not need to know that," Proster said, "If he believes it is magic that is fine. Overall, we can stay here until we hear from the scouts that the army is headed our way."

"I will let the men know," Herwin said. Proster nodded. Herwin left Proster alone.

After a few more minutes of sitting there, Proster got up and went into his tent for the night.

The next morning Proster sat and watched as the farmers came out of the town walls. They were still nervous going passed Proster's men, but they went out to their fields anyway. There were more farmers today that went out to the fields. It looked like they were getting ready to harvest. Though Proster noticed that each farmer worked his own field and any help he had was his own sons. Most of the sons seemed to be twelve or under. The farmers were not all older men, but they did not have any young men helping them. Proster wondered whether that had something to do with the army's recruitment program or whether all of them just decided to leave.

Proster saw Clovis walking passed. Proster met his eyes and signalled for him to come over. Clovis has been one of the men that had gone with the traders into the town and had been collecting information. Clovis walked over to where Proster was sitting.

"What can I do for you?" Clovis asked.

"What is with the lack of young men helping in the fields?" Proster asked.

"The king of Batend has things set up so that there is always a farmer per allocated land for a farm," Clovis answered, "Once all the fields have farmers, then all the rest of the men are taken to the capital city. Some return as guards, but never the ones that were removed from the town. The rest goes into the army that the king of Batend has. The program has been in effect since the king took the throne. Now he is focusing on supplies to the capital and making sure that the people are not selling it to anyone else."

"Does not sound good," Proster said.

"No one complains," Clovis replied.

"Why complain when you are still alive and still semi free," Proster said.

Clovis shrugged.

"Thank you for the information," Proster said. Clovis went back to what he was doing. Proster went back to watching the farmers.

When mid-morning came Proster was still watching the farmers. Many of them were trying to harvest the wheat. They were doing what they could do alone and they were going at it very slowly. It seemed to Proster that leaving one farmer for allocated chunk of land was a foolish way to do things especially if there is any problem with the harvest. If the weather for the year was worse than the farmers would never make it and the whole harvest would be lost. Then the residents would starve and the king could not get food for the cities.

Garrick sat down in the dirt next to Proster. Proster nodded that he noticed Garrick`s presence, but did not say anything. Garrick did not say anything immediately.

One of the farmers in the fields closest to where the men were camped was having problems. It looked like something had broke or something similar was wrong. He was one of the farmers working without help. Proster guessed that he did not have a son in the right age range that could help him. The farmer struggled for several minutes. Some of the men that were practicing nearby stopped their fight. They went over to the farmer and one of them stepped away from the group. He spoke to the farmer for several minutes. Then the group went on to the field and started to help the farmer. The farmer seemed to appreciate the help as he went back to work.

"I was wondering about how to deal with men if they got bored," Garrick said, "That scene gives a good suggestion."

"If the town needs help with anything else the men can help with that as well," Proster said, "It helps them not to be as nervous about us. It also creates goodwill."

"What if they do not want the help?" Garrick asked.

"Then they do not have to have our help," Proster answered. Garrick nodded. Both men were quiet as they watched the men help the farmer. Several other farmers stopped their work briefly to look at the men helping the farmer. Some looked like they would not mind the help and others just shook their heads before going back to work.

"I will send some men around," Garrick said. He got to his feet and left Proster alone.

A few minutes went passed before another group of men left the camp and headed towards one of the farms. One of the men approached the farmer. He spoke to the farmer for several minutes and then the group started to help the farmer. This was repeated multiple times with Proster's men and farmers. Most of the farmers are willing to accept help, but a few refused the help.

Proster watched the farmers and his men until after lunch. Then he put on his armour and found some men that were practicing. They let him join them.

By the end of the second day of Proster and his men camping outside the town walls, the harvest had been taken in and the farmers were putting their fields to bed for the winter. Within the same amount of time people in the town let Proster's men help them. There were still some that refused the help. Algernon would talk to the people after Proster's men had left and tell them what the king of Batend would do if he found out. The townspeople that were willing to accept help did not seem to be swayed by that idea.

Proster's men appreciated having something to do, even if it meant working in the fields. There were still some that practiced their fighting skills rather than helping the townspeople. Proster joined them, because if he so much as suggested to someone that he might like to help out he was given strange looks. Proster chose not to deal with that.

The evening of that third day, Proster was sitting in the usual spot outside his tent. The farmers had all gone back into the town walls and his men were all back in camp. Herwin was squatting nearby Proster and explaining what the scouts had reported back. Proster was only half listening as he stared across the fields. The sun was getting close to the horizon and purple and pinks were mixing with the blue of the sky.

Proster became aware that Herwin had stopped talking. Proster glanced at him and saw that Herwin was looking toward the town. Proster looked in that direction. Algernon was coming toward them.

"I will tell you the rest later," Herwin said. He straightened up and walked away.

Algernon stopped at what he considered a respectable distance and bowed.

"I need to speak with you, Prince Proster," Algernon said.

"Have a seat," Proster pointed to the patch of dirt across from him. This time Algernon sat without hesitation.

"What is it that you wish to speak with me about?" Proster asked.

"Your men," Algernon answered, "I know that they think they are helping, but they are just making things worse for us once you have left. It would be better if your men stayed in the camp and left the people alone."

"I thought about doing that," Proster said, "but then I thought about how bored my men get when they have nothing to do. At least if they are helping people they are doing something productive. There are some things they could do that would be a lot less productive. Since the townspeople have welcomed the help, I have decided to let my men do such and even encouraged them. I doubt that the king of Batend would destroy the village just because my men helped them. He needs the farmers to work the land and he appreciates getting the harvest in early. The town did not welcome us. The town did not invite us into the country. We attacked the town and moved into the area against your will. You are the only one that might feel the anger of the king. After all bureaucrats are the most easily replaced of all the people. So, you are only trying to protect your own skin, but I am sure that you will think up something when you are interrogated."

Algernon had paled. His mouth was opening and closing as if he was trying to come up with an angry retort.

"You may go," Proster said. Algernon stood up. His mouth was still moving, but he bowed anyway. Then he walked back into the town wall.

"He really does not believe we can defeat the Batend army," Herwin said as he squatted down near Proster again.

"He has been thoroughly convinced that the Batend army is undefeatable," Proster replied, "He is easily convinced by those with more power than he has."

"And that is why you act like royalty for him," Herwin said.

"With him it works well," Proster said.

A farmer came out of the town walls. He went to the nearest warrior. He asked the warrior a question. The warrior answered and pointed toward Proster.

"I wonder if the mayor convinced someone else to come out and plea the case for not helping the people," Herwin said.

"Maybe," Proster said.

The farmer came over to where Proster and Herwin were.

"I was told you are the leader," the farmer said.

"I am the leader," Proster said as he stood up, "My name is Proster." Proster offered his hand. Herwin also stood up, but he took a step back as if he did not want to appear to be in on the conversation.

"I am Jorrin," the farmer answered. He shook Proster's hand.

"Is there something that you need, Jorrin?" Proster asked.

"I just wanted to come out and thank you and your men for helping us," Jorrin answered, "Without the help it would have taken much longer to take in the harvest. Two years ago we would have helped each other out and done each farm in turn, but now each of us is worried about our own farms. If we do not get the harvest off our own fields in time we are punished and it does not matter if we were slow because we are helping other people. Last year the harvest took longer than it has ever taken before with each worried about himself than the community. Algernon is so concerned about his reputation and pleasing the king that he will not defend us. There is nothing we can do, but hope for change. I know you are here to fight the army and perhaps take down the king. I hope you succeed and that you manage to take him out. Anything would be better than the current problems coming out of the capital."

"Algernon does not seem to think we have much chance of defeating the army," Proster said.

"The army is not going to be a problem," Jorrin said, "It is made up of men. It might be larger, but it is still men. It is once you reach the capital that you will face the real problem."

"What is that?" Proster asked.

"The king is the one on the throne and the ruler of Batend, but he has a wizard in his employment," Jorrin said, "That is where the rumours of invincibility come from. If you kill the wizard than the king will be easier to kill."

"How do you know this?" Herwin said.

"The king and his wizard came through two years ago after the harvest," Jorrin answered, "We were introduced to both of them as they showed us what would happen if we disobeyed them. Algernon is not likely to tell you any of this because he thinks he can please the king and the king will give him a position in the capital. I have not heard of any positions in the capital aside from being in the army, but I am just a farmer and not privy to all the news reports from the capital."

"Thank you for telling us all this," Proster said, "I do not know how well my men will do against the army, but if I can do something to change your situation I will."

"Thank you," Jorrin said. Jorrin turned and headed back into the town wall.

"The truth?" Herwin asked.

"He was genuine and gave no indication of lying," Proster said, "I would say that he is telling us the truth as he knows it. And most of what he knows is based on what he has seen for himself."

"So, we will have a wizard to contend with when we reach the capital," Herwin said.

"It appears so," Proster replied, "We will deal with that when we reach the capital. First, we have an army to fight."

"I do not think the army will be a problem," Herwin said, "It is like Jorrin said, it is just men."

It was the third day camped out when one of the men spotted a man headed their direction on a horse. Proster was called. The horse was coming from the direction of Grackle, not from in Batend. As Proster watched it come closer he saw that it wore the colours of one of his father's messengers. Once most of the men realized that, they went back to whatever they had been doing before the horse was spotted.

The messenger rode into camp and to where Proster was standing and waiting. The messenger got off his horse and stood before Proster. Despite the height difference, Proster wanted to laugh at the man's air of self-importance.

"I come with a message from King Thedious of Grackle," the messenger announced with his chest puffed out.

"And here I thought you might be bringing us a message of surrender for the king of Batend," Proster said, "A pity."

"King Thedious demands that you stop your attack on Batend and return home," the messenger said.

"Or what?" Proster asked, "He has no army to send after me because I lead the only fighting force he has. I am not a child that simply obeys without question. I also know that I need to feed my men and our animals. He was not willing to give me enough food to do that. I will continue my attack on Batend despite his demands to the otherwise. It he does not like it then he can come and discuss the matter with me himself."

"King Thedious will not be happy," the messenger's voice had a slight menacing quality to it.

"Go return to him with what I said," Proster said, "Otherwise, you will be my men's next meal." Proster pulled out his sword and put the tip against the messenger's chest.

The messenger paled. He took a step back before getting on his horse. The messenger turned the horse around and started back towards Grackle. Before getting out of sight he glanced back at Proster. Proster smiled and waved. The messenger spurred his horse to go faster.

THE SECOND BATTLE, THIS TIME AGAINST THE ACTUAL ARMY

Proster and his men had been camped outside the town for about a week when the word came back from the scouts that the army of Batend was headed their direction. The day that word arrived Proster had his men pack up camp and say good bye to the residents of the town. Once the camp was cleaned up to the point that it looked like no one had been camped there for a week, Proster lead his men away from the town and deeper into the Batend countryside.

Over the course of the week Proster, Herwin and Garrick had been studying a map of Batend. They determined that the army was likely to go passed a town that was a three days march from the town where Proster's men had been camped. When the scouts send back word they said that the army was headed for that town. Proster figured that if they started marching toward the town that his men would meet up with the Batend army in a large open area that was about half way between the two of them. And that would be the best place for the battle.

Proster marched his men to the field. They stopped to rest at regular intervals, but they still reached the field before the other army did. Proster had them set up on one side of the field. And there they waited.

It was the next morning after they arrived at the field the scouts arrived with word that the army was headed their way. Proster and his men got ready for battle. When the sound of the army could be heard they were in the formation that they used to attack. Proster stood at the front of his men with Herwin on one side of him and Garrick on the other side of him. The rest of the men were in longer rows behind them.

"That sounds strange," Garrick said as they stood and waited, "It does not sound like men marching. Although there is something marching towards us."

"Unless the men are wearing soft soled boots," Herwin said.

Both of them were silent as the Batend army came into sight. It looked to Proster as if the king of Batend sent most of his army if not all of it. Proster figured there to be two thousand. The army kept coming until they were a spear's throw away from Proster and his men. There was a ripple of surprise that went through the men behind Proster, but each man also readied himself for the coming battle.

Proster looked out over the battle field. There were lines of snarling orcs and they had all been given a sword and armour. They stood in military formation with their black faces toward Proster and his group of a hundred warriors.

"No wonder the king of Batend does not have to worry about his army deserting him," Herwin commented.

"There must be two thousand of them," Garrick said.

"You know the saying," Herwin said, "You start with two orcs and the next thing you know you have two dozen to feed."

"If we are fighting orcs, where are the soldiers the king of Batend keeps demanding of his people?" Proster's voice was quieter, but both his advisors heard him and glanced at each other. Proster's comment was worrying, because if they were facing orcs then the human army was coming later, not to mention anything else the king of Batend had under his command.

One of the orcs stepped out of the formation. It lifted is sword over it head and gave a loud snarl. The rest of the orcs started forward and passed him. Proster braced himself with his sword at ready. As soon as the first one was in range Proster started swinging. The orcs were faster than any Proster had ever encountered. They were as fast as humans that had been trained to fight. Proster instantly found himself with three or four of the orcs surrounding him and trying to hack at him with their swords. He was just able to keep up with them. With an army of men Proster would not have taken on more than two or three at a time, but this time he had no choice. From the brief glances he could afford his men were having the same problem that he was.

He parried and slashed, dodging between slashes by his enemies. Proster put his sword through one of the orcs and quickly pulled it out to parry the swing from another orc. The one orc fell to its knees and then down onto its stomach, but before it finished dying a new orc had joined the fight with Proster. Proster dodged one attack as he parried another and finished with a punch to the head of the third orc. He freed up his sword in time to take the head off the orc closest to him and then dodge another attack. He parried another swing before ducking the throwing axe, which end up buried in the orc's chest.

Each time one orc was down another stepped into the fight to take its place as if there was a large group of them waiting just outside the fight for an opening. Proster received several scratches and a stab wound to his right shoulder, but he kept fighting. Occasionally he would catch a glimpse of the rest of his men and saw that they were dealing with the same thing that he was. But he could not tell much else before the next attack would have to be parried or dodged.

This fight lasted a good portion of the day and into the evening. As the sunlight disappeared over the horizon and the moon's light was what was giving illumination to the battle field. Proster noticed that the number of orcs was starting to decrease. As the number decreased the survivors fought harder. Proster found that now that there were only two fighting him he was having a harder time to dodge and parry both of them. There was even a few times when he was not sure that he was not going to be killed by an orc.

The moon was over head making it seem closer to noon than the middle of the night. Proster parried a sword swing before dodging the swing from behind him. He spun around and thrust his sword at the orc. Orc was not fast enough to block the sword and it went straight through the orc's chest. Proster pulled out the sword and turned back to other orc. He parried the sword swing that was headed his direction. The orc was quick to pull its sword away and bring it down hard again. Proster felt the vibrations of the hit go down his sword to his hands. It hurt, but he managed to keep a hold on his sword. The orc pulled away and brought the sword down again before Proster could fully recover. Proster's sword dropped out of his hand and he had to jump back to avoid the orc's swing. He managed to get out of sword range, but Poster slipped on a corpse of an orc and it caused him to go backwards. Proster ended up on his back with the orc coming at him. He rolled to his right before the orc could bring down its sword again. Proster found the handle of the dead orc's sword as he was rolling. He grabbed it as he got to his feet. The orc came at him again. Proster charged and put the sword through the orc's stomach before stepping out of the way. The orc fell forward and did not move.

Proster picked up his own sword and looked around the battle field. Most of his men were still battling orcs, but those were the only orcs left on the battle field. Proster could also see some of his own men lying among the corpses, but he pushed that thought out of head for the moment. He would have to deal with it later.

Garrick was nearby fighting one orc. Proster headed cross the space to where the fight was. He was just about there when Garrick fell to his knees and the orc was about to run him through with a sword. Proster swung and decapitated the orc before it could finished its swing. The body dropped with the sword still in its hand. Garrick looked up at Proster. He was splattered with dirt and the black blood of orcs. There was also some blood for scratches he had received. Proster offered Garrick his hand. Garrick accepted the help getting to his feet.

"We were not prepared for this," Garrick said looking around. He started to his left. Proster followed him.

"I knew that the king of Batend had a wizard in his employment, but I had not heard anything about orcs," Proster said, "If I had known I would have set up this fight differently. The worst time to fight orcs is at night when they are strongest."

Garrick stopped and looked down. Herwin was lying in among the other corpse in the grass. Garrick bent down and checked for a pulse.

"Is he still alive?" Proster asked.

"I am getting a pulse, but it is weak," Garrick answered. He turned Herwin from his side to his back. Herwin groaned, but did not wake up. There was a blade of an orc sword stuck in Herwin's stomach. Garrick pulled it out and blood started pumping out of the wound. Proster took a vial out of his pouch and handed it to Garrick. Garrick took it and opened it. He put one drop on the wound and a second drop into Herwin's mouth. Then he handed the vial back to Proster. The wound closed up until it was just a fresh scar.

"He'll be fine," Proster said tucking the vial back into his pouch, "Let's keep going."

"Okay," Garrick said. He straightened up and they started forward.

As the two of them went across the field they looked for fallen men as well as helping in any battle they came near. Slowly other men joined them. There were six bodies pulled out and some of the men started piling the orc corpses to one side. Most of the men being pulled out were dead. There were two that were still alive and were saved through the liquid in the vial. The dead were lined up in their own place. The injured were tended to in a different area that was off the battle field.

When the cleanup was finished, there were eight of Poster's men that were dead, a dozen injured enough to require attention, and two thousand five hundred bodies of orcs. Proster had his men set up camp on the other side of the field from the direction they had come from. It did not take long to set up camp even though many could not help. The injured were taken care of and the dead were left out to be buried in the morning. Proster supervised it all and stayed up until everything was cleaned up. Finally he gave some warriors watch and went to bed. He was grateful as he sank into sleep.

"Proster," Garrick's voice was loud and too close by. Proster opened his eyes before the wave exhaustion hit him. Whatever sleep he had gotten was not enough according to his body. Proster sat up and looked at where Garrick was standing inside the flap to the tent. Garrick seemed slightly spooked. The flame in lantern in Garrick's hand flickered.

"Yes?" Proster asked.

"You need to see this," Garrick answered. Proster got out of bed and strapped on his sword. Garrick left the tent and Proster followed him out. There were several men standing around. It looked like they had all be woken up by something and it was not good. Herwin was standing nearby. He was still pale and looked like he needed some rest, but he was standing.

"This way," Garrick said leading the way. Proster followed. Herwin went with them.

"How are you doing?" Proster asked Herwin.

"Like I need to sleep for a month," Herwin answered, "Thank you for saving me."

"It would be difficult to run this army without you," Proster said. Herwin nodded.

Garrick was headed for the battle field and where all the corpses were. Proster could not think of what would spook him so much that would be there. Unless of course, the orcs were getting up, but Proster figured that he would be moving at a faster pace if that were true. As they got closer Proster could see the pile of bodies on the field, but could not see reason for alarm. Garrick stopped by a body that was lying a little bit of a distance away from the pile and moved the lantern closer to it. Proster stopped and looked down at the body. The face of the corpse was human. It was a young man, but it could not have been one of Proster's warriors because he was perhaps fifteen, maybe younger. The armour he wore was that of the orc army of Batend. There was black blood on the armour around the hole in the armour, but the dried blood underneath was red.

"All the rest of the bodies are the same," Garrick said when Proster looked up at him, "They have orc armour and orc blood on them, but they are human."

"We just butchered a bunch of children," Herwin said. His voice shook and his face had gone whiter.

"We fought an army of orcs," Proster said, "It was the king of Batend and his wizard that send an army of children into battle as orcs."

"I thought that would be impossible," Herwin said, "That big a spell."

"There are several transformation spells that would do it," Proster said, "And it would not have to a large spell all at once but smaller spells over time. As the young men show up for the recruitment they would be transformed. Then they would not desert the army or disobey the king. And when they die the spell goes away leaving a pile of children."

"And we feel guilty about murdering those children," Herwin said.

"What do we do with the bodies?" Garrick asked, "We cannot just leave them here and we cannot track down their families to return them."

"We bury them," Proster said, "Starting tomorrow. Each grave will be marked with a sword and helmet. This battle field will be a grave yard for them. Hopefully they will rest without being disturbed further."

"Their families will not get to rest," Herwin said.

"That is the price we all must pay for other people's evil," Proster said.

"I will get the men on it tomorrow morning," Garrick said.

"The day after we will continue our march for the capital," Proster said, "But we do things slightly differently. We no longer kill our opponents, but subdue them. Perhaps we can avoid this kind of horror next time."

Herwin and Garrick nodded. Proster stated back toward his tent. After a moment Garrick and Herwin started back to camp as well.

When Proster woke up it was mid-afternoon based on the amount of light from outside his tent. Proster changed into something less blood splattered before going outside.

The camp was quiet and there was no one around. Proster went to where he could see the field. Everyone was out there digging graves and placing bodies in the ground. Proster stopped long enough to get something to eat before going out and joining them.

His men were too busy to notice that he was one of the people helping. They were so focused on their task. By the time someone realized that he was out there getting dirty he was down in a hole digging it out to the appropriate depth. One of the men tried to protest Proster working in the dirt, but no one else would let him.

It was early evening when the final body was put into the ground and covered up. Each of the graves was marked with a sword buried half way up to the hilt and a helmet placed on the sword. It looked like rows of crosses. Proster's men that died had also been buried. Their bodies were marked with wooden crosses. The rest of the evening was spent around the camp. That night there was no air of victory, just the oppressive feel of depression. The horrors of the battle, of losing some of their own, and of what the other side truly was were being felt in every man's mind and heart.

Proster faced his own mental battles, but knew he could not let them distract him. He spent the evening thinking over everything he knew about the capital city, the king of Batend, the king's wizard, and the land between the current camp and the capital. He went over the plan that he, Herwin and Garrick had come up with before they understood the whole situation. And he thought about what changes would need to be made. The scouts here reported that there were no more large groups headed their direction. It seemed almost like the king of

Batend assumed that his army would succeed and that it would not need the help of any more troops. Proster hoped that no more troops would be sent, but know that he and his men would have to be careful.

THE CAPITAL CITY OF BATEND AND THE THIRD BATTLE IN THE WAR FOR BATEND.

The next morning Proster sent a handful of men into the nearby town to get some supplies while all the rest of the men worked on taking down the camp. By the time the men came back, the camp was packed up and everyone was ready to go. Once the supplies were packed away, Proster gave the order for the men to get ready to march. The men gathered and Proster took the lead position. They started to march.

They headed directly for the capital city of Batend. Staying on the main roads, they avoided trampling anyone's field. They only stopped near towns if they needed supplies. When they stopped for the night, Proster had them sleep near each other in the open with regular watches. This was because although the spies kept sending back reports that there were no forces headed they direction, small groups of orcs would appear and start attacking them. This slowed down the march as did finding trees to tie the orcs to that would prevent them from getting free.

It took a week and a half for Proster and his men to reach a field near the capital where they made camp again.

The capital city of Batend was surrounded by a stone wall. The wall was too tall to climb and was thick enough for guards to walk along the top of them. The whole city was within the walls, but the castle took up a quarter of the space and was situated farthest from the front gate. The walls met with the walls of the castle and at the back the two were together, making no room between the two at the back. There were human guards that walked along the top of the walls and guarded the front gates. It looked like an impenetrable fortress.

Outside the stone walls of the city was a few open areas, such as where Proster and his men were camped, but most of it was forest. There was a road that went passed the front gate of the capital city, which received regular traffic, but there were no other roads that went to the city. The back of the city was just forest. The road headed passed most of the forest and on the next town.

Proster had his men go into the city in groups of twos and threes through the front gate to check out the town. Over three days they came back with enough information to make a map of the city, but the castle had a gate to get inside. Inside was also where the army was as well as anything else that was necessary for the castle. It was like the king wanted an extra layer of defence if the city was over run. And the king did not hold court for the people to come in with their complaints so there was no way to sneak in that way. Any goods that went into the castle were taken as far as the gate and then the guards took it from there and the people never set foot inside the gates. From everything that was coming back it was impossible to get into the castle without an invitation and Proster doubted that the king would issue him and his men an invitation.

Proster kept sending men into the city to gather information. He hoped that someone would come up with something that would be useful.

Proster was sitting outside his tent studying the wall that surrounded the city. It was as solid as it had been when they set up camp near it a week ago. No plans had yet come to Proster as to how to get into the castle and he did not want to take over the town if he could not get into the castle, especially since he knew that there was a wizard inside that castle.

Herwin came over to where Proster was sitting.

"The latest set of men is heading into the city," Herwin said.

"Okay," Proster said.

"I am not sure what they are supposed to bring back that the last group did not," Herwin said.

"Anything that will help us," Proster said.

"I told them to see what they could get for supplies while they are in there," Herwin said, "Unfortunately, Garrick did not have much money he could give them. Garrick and I talked and he figures that at the rate we are going we will be out of supplies in two days. At which point we will be out of food and money to buy food. If you are going to come up with the wealth from this venture I would suggest that you come up with enough to feed us until you have an idea on how to get into the castle."

"I will work on it," Proster said. Herwin stayed where he was, but neither of them spoke. Five minutes went passed. Ten minutes went passed. Fifteen minutes went passed. Twenty minutes went passed.

"Is there anything else?" Proster asked Herwin.

"I would suggest a walk," Herwin answered, "You have been sitting in that position for the last two days. It is making the men nervous."

"And where do you think I should walk?" Poster asked looking at Herwin.

"If you walk around the wall of the city you can still stare at it while contemplating your plan," Herwin suggested.

"I will think about it," Proster said. Herwin shrugged and then walked away. Proster went back to staring at the wall.

His mind was still trying to come up with a plan, but his mind also was going over Herwin's words. He glanced around at his own men once in a while. Proster found that Herwin's words were true. His men were starting to get nervous.

Proster got to his feet. He stretched the kinks out and then started to walk. He headed around the back of the castle. The trees were closer together and the walking was a little rough. It was also difficult to see the wall in some places. Proster moved so that he was walking right next to the wall. None of the guards seemed to be out today. Proster would stop and study the wall, but it was the same stone all the way around. It was still the impenetrable stone that was starting to taunt him. Proster reached the back of the city, where the wall was also part of the castle. He stopped and looked up at the wall. He expected it to have no more solutions to his problem than any other chunk of wall. But instead he saw a door.

The door was made of wood and was about a hundred and fifty metres straight up from where Proster was standing at the bottom of the wall. Proster had heard of such doors. It was a way to send unwanted guests out the back way so that they never came back. His father had removed the one from his castle and replaced it with stones. Many other kings did something similar, but a few just locked the inside. After all there was no way anyone could get to them from the outside. Proster looked around and saw that there was no bones or other signs of dead bodies. He figured that someone must clean up after the king.

An idea came to Proster. It slowly unveiled itself in his mind. Proster smiled as he saw it all. There were a few holes, but those could be worked out. His mind kept going over this idea as he headed back toward the camp.

When he was out of the forest and could see the camp he noticed that there was something going on. He walked over to the group that was talking. Garrick and Herwin were both there as well as one of the groups that had gone into the city that morning. None of them were aware if Proster as he walked over to them. The men had guard uniforms with them.

"We were not doing anything," Loic was apparently answering Garrick's question, "They chased us half a block when we stepped into an alley way they followed us. They tried to beat us and instead we knocked them out. Herve and I decided that we should take their uniforms. Maybe it would help us get into the castle, or at least scout out the inside."

"I am not sure how much help the uniforms would be," Garrick said, "Especially since we do not know how many guards there are and whether they would know each other."

"But they can be useful once inside the castle," Proster said. The last part of the idea clicked into place. Everyone turned toward him.

"You have figured out how to get into the castle?" Herwin asked.

"Yes," Proster answered, "The walk helped a lot. The uniforms will give us more freedom once we are inside."

"We only got two of them," Loic said.

"That is okay," Proster said, "If should be enough. Only two need to get into the castle. All the rest will be attacking the front gate."

"That is useless," Garrick said, "There is no way to get into the castle from that side. The king of Batend can just sit there and sent troops."

"But he will be watching to see when he has to send more troops," Proster said, "That gives the men that sneak into the castle the time to get in and open the gates. The frontal assault will work as a distraction only, not as the full attack."

"When are we going to be attacking the capital city of Batend?" Herwin asked.

"Tomorrow," Proster answered before turning to Garrick, "What have we got for rope?"

The sun was just rising above the trees as Proster and the four men that were with him started into the trees. Garrick, Vila, Loic and Menawa were following him as he led the way back to the place in the wall. All the rest of the men were gathering in front of the main gates to begin their frontal assault. Herwin was leading them. They already knew they were going to get through the front gates without difficulty, it would be the castle gates that stop them.

Proster and Garrick were dressed up in the uniforms that had been stolen. They would be the only ones to enter the castle. The other three would remain on the ground outside. They would make sure that it was possible to go back out that door if necessary.

They reached the wall below the door as the sounds of fighting at the front gates could be heard.

"I know they are supposed to be making a lot of noise," Garrick said, "But that sounds like a lot more than necessary."

"I just hope that the king of Batend can hear it as well," Proster said.

The five stopped and Vila unpacked everything he needed. The other four got out of the way as he loaded the bolt into the crossbow. Then he aimed carefully and pulled the trigger. The bolt went up and embedded itself in the wood of the door. Vila gave it a good tug and the bolt stayed in place.

"It's ready," Vila said.

"Okay," Proster said, "Remember to keep your eyes out for any trouble."

"We will," Loic said.

Proster started climbing up the rope. When he reached the top he found that there was a ledge that he could stand on. He tried the door and found that it opened easily. Proster opened it enough that he could stick his head inside. There was no one in the hall. He stepped inside and let the rope go.

A few minutes later Garrick reached the door and Proster helped him inside. Garrick let the rope go and Proster closed the door behind them.

"Any chance that you have any idea which way to go?" Garrick asked looking left and then right. Both directions looked the same with stone walls, stone floors, and stone ceiling. Proster stood there and listened for a minute. There was some noise coming from the right.

"That way," Proster said pointing left.

"Why?" Garrick asked.

"There are no sounds coming from this direction," Proster said as he started down the left corridor. Garrick followed. This corridor curved so it was just about impossible to see what was ahead even when staying near the outside wall. There was also no doors or windows along it at any point. As they went along Proster thought that the floor might be sloping upwards, but he was not sure. If it was sloping upwards it was doing so at a very small angle.

They had been going along this corridor for a while when Proster saw an opening ahead. He signalled it to Garrick and they slowed down and moved slower. The opening turned out to be the end of the corridor. Any thing further was open air. Proster and Garrick stopped. They could hear voices from below. They dropped to their stomachs before getting any closer to the edge. At the edge they peered over the side.

Below them was the court room of the king of Batend, and he was currently sitting on the throne. There were several guards standing around and well as some servants. The room itself was bare. The throne was on a dais with red and gold curtains behind it. The throne matched the curtains. There was a carpet, also red and gold, that went from the throne to the door that was across the room for it. There were no other decorations in the throne room at all. The door appeared to be the only way into and out of the throne room. A man in a blue robe with silver runes on it stood to one side of the dais. He stood apart from all the others in the room. He appeared to be staring at the wall and mulling over something important. He had a staff in one hand that had a crystal in the top.

Proster noted that some of the guards were orcs and some were human. Though they all seemed to be standing around as if the king of Batend needed an audience, but did not want anyone around that might cause him trouble. Though at the moment the king of Batend was just sitting on his throne reading a scroll of parchment and not addressing anyone.

The doors opened. Proster saw that it was a hallway outside the throne room and there appeared to be guards on either side of that door. A human guard stepped into the throne room.

"Your majesty," the guard's words echoed in the hall.

"What is it?" the king of Batend's voice held contempt for being addressed by someone of lower rank.

"The city gate is being attacked," the guard answered.

"By who?" the king of Batend asked.

"By close to a hundred men," the guard answered, "Their leader has yet to be identified and no one has spoken to any of the men."

"Send out some of the troops to fight them off when they get in the castle gate, if they get in the city gate," the king of Batend seemed bored at the whole idea, "Close the gate to the castle. Let no one in or out."

"Yes, your highness," the guard replied. Then he turned and left the throne room. The king of Batend signalled the rest of the guards in the throne room and they all left. The wizard was the only one who did not move.

"Would you like me to cast a spell?" the wizard asked.

"That is not necessary," the king of Batend answered, "The guards can take care of the nuisances."

"Yes, your highness," the wizard bowed, "I will be in the tower if you need me." The wizard left by the door to the throne room. The king of Batend went back to reading his scroll of parchment.

Proster tapped Garrick on the shoulder and they moved back from the edge. They got to their feet and then went farther down the hallway.

"The attack is working like you planned it," Garrick said.

"Yes, it is," Proster said, "You go get the king of Batend and hold him hostage."

"What about you?" Garrick asked.

"I am going to find the wizard," Proster answered.

"That is going to be dangerous," Garrick said.

"I know," Proster said, "Now once you have the king of Batend hostage barrack yourself in the throne room. There does not seem to be any other way out of there."

"What happens if the wizard kills you?" Garrick asked.

"Then it is up to you and Herwin to finish the takeover of the kingdom," Proster said, "I am sure between the two of you one would make a good king." Proster headed down the corridor. Garrick stood there for a minute before following.

This direction went down as the other had sloped up. Again there were no doors or windows, except the door they came in through. At the end of the corridor was a door that was open just a little bit. Proster looked through the crack between the door and the door frame. It was just another corridor, but there were more people out there this time. Most of the guards were headed in one direction and the servants in the other. Proster stepped into the corridor. He started in the direction that the servants were going. He heard Garrick coming out of the door and going the other direction.

No one even looked at Proster a second time despite the fact that he was going the wrong direction. The fact that he wore a guard 's uniform was enough for them. He followed this corridor until it came to a junction. The right direction must have led to the courtyard because guards were going down that hallway. The centre one was where all the servants were headed. The left on was practically empty of all people. Proster headed down there. It was not long before he felt the sloping sensation again. It was sloping upward. At the end of this corridor was a door that led into a study that must have been for the king of Batend, but looked unused, and a staircase. The staircase was used. In fact Proster could still hear the sound of someone going up the stairs. Proster started up, but he did so as quietly as he could.

The staircase was wide enough for a large person to go through, but it was like the stairs were twisting around a pole in their centre. There was no way to see anyone above you or below you. Once Proster had turned around enough that he could no longer see the hallway below the light faded as well. There were no torches or lamps, or any other light source along these stairs. The person's footsteps above Proster did not seem to be having much trouble. Proster slowly felt his way along.

It seemed to take forever as Proster made his way up the stairs. It was dark and he was trying to be quiet. The person above him was moving at a much faster pace. Finally the footsteps above him stopped. Then there was the sound of a door opening and closing. Proster continued up, through this time not as quiet as before.

He came around a turn and found light coming through a window above him. At the top of the stairs was a flat area before the door, where someone could stop and look out the window if they wanted to. Proster finally reached this flat surface and stopped. He looked out the window. The whole city was spread out before him. He was in the tallest tower of the castle. He could see his men were at the castle gates and were fighting the guards in front of them. They had been joined by a group of men. From the distance it looked to Proster that his men had been joined by some of the residents of the city.

Proster turned back to the door and took out his sword. He took a deep breath before opening the door and stepping inside. The room was full of shelves that had bottles, pots, glasses, and loose spell components. There was a large space in one end of the room with a rune painted on the floor. The other end of the room had a large table that filled it. The table was covered with all sorts of small objects. There was also a book opened up to a page that the wizard was standing behind the table studying.

"Has his highness changed his mind about the attackers?" the wizard did not even bother to look up at Proster.

"I would not know," Proster answered, "I have not met him yet."

The wizard looked up at Proster and the sword in his hand.

"You are not here on his orders," the wizard said.

"I am Prince Proster of Grackle," Proster said, "I come of my own will."

"I see," the wizard said, "You will die of your own will too." The wizard's hand came up and he threw a fireball at Proster. Proster dodged out of the way and then rolled out of the way of the lightening that came his direction.

"You are a very foolish person to come up here," the wizard said as he gathered a bigger fireball into his hand.

Proster did not respond as he started to get closer to the wizard. He had to duck the next fireball. The wizard picked up a bag off the desk. He reached into it and pulled out a handful of something. Proster backed off as the wizard threw a handful of dust into the air while saying a spell. Proster was too far away from the wizard for any of the dust to settle on him. The spell did not affect him. The wizard cursed before waving his hand. That caused the dust to burst into flame. The flame created a bearer between Proster and the wizard's desk.

Proster hesitated as he asseted the situation. The wizard laughed.

"Really you thought it was that easy to just come in here and kill me," the wizard said.

"No," Proster replied, "I did not think anything like that." He walked toward the wizard. Reaching the fire he stepped over the line and the flames did not touch him.

"So you have some protection," the wizard said, "But now that I know that it is just that much easier to get rid of you." The wizard signalled one of the objects behind him. A flanged mace raised itself off the shelf behind the wizard and headed in the direction of Proster. Proster's ducked the weapon's first charge, but before it could turn around to try again Proster was back up and grabbed the handle with his right hand. The weapon did not fight Proster anymore, but become just a normal inanimate weapon.

The wizard looked like he was starting to get angry. He picked up his staff from where it was resting against the wall.

"I will show you real power," the wizard snarled. He blasted Proster. The blast of power sent Proster across the room to crash into the back wall. But the wizard continued the flow of power trapping Proster against the wall. Proster gasped for air as the force of the power was crushing him to the wall.

"See, you are not as strong as you think," the wizard said as he moved out from behind the table, "I am more powerful than you thought. A lesson you will never get to learn is that you should not mess with wizards when all you have going for you is a minor dispel." The wizard came closer to Proster and put more power into crushing him. The flanged mace dropped from Proster's hand, but he managed to keep a hold on his sword. The wizard laughed as he continued to crush Proster with power.

Then the laughter stopped as Proster dropped from the wall and rolled forward. While the wizard was trying to stop the current spell and find another one Proster buried his sword into the wizard's gut up to the hilt.

"I have faced wizards before," Proster told the wizard, who was now staring at him in shock, "The best offense against them is to let them think they are winning." Proster pulled his sword out and let the wizard fall to the floor. Proster wiped his blade off on the wizard's robe before leaving the room.

He stopped at the window and saw that the battle for the castle gate was still on going. His men and the town residents had the upper hand, but the gate was still closed and would be until he or Garrick opened them. Proster headed back down the tower stairs.

Back at the junction of the four hallways he headed back down the hallway that he had the door he had come in through. He went passed the door and continued down the hallway. It was much quieter this time. There were no guards and all the servants seemed to be off somewhere. There were still some servants, but none of them even glanced in his direction.

The end of this hallway led to a larger corridor. This one Proster recognized as leading to the throne room. At each end of the hallway was a large fancy door. Proster turned right into the corridor. He went down to the door at the end of the hallway. He opened it enough that he could stick his head out.

There were a couple squads standing in the courtyard watching the gates. There were three gates. One straight ahead, one to the left and one to the right. The squadrons were waiting with their weapons ready. Most were orcs. Proster briefly wondered how to break that spell as he pulled his head back inside. He closed the door before heading back down the hallway.

Proster knocked on the door at this end of the corridor. A moment passed before the door opened. Garrick was standing there and opened the door enough that Proster could step inside. This room was the throne room. The king of Batend lying on the stone floor near the dais. The king of Batend had been hogtied and gagged.

Proster stepped into the room and closed the door behind him. Garrick looked up at him.

"I did not have a choice," Garrick said, "He did not want to stay still and then when I tied him up he would not stop talking."

"It should be fine for the moment," Proster said.

"What happened with the wizard?" Garrick asked.

"He thought I should not be too much trouble to take out," Proster answered, "And did not expect me to be able to run him through with my sword."

"I guess it is true that wizards cannot sense your sword," Garrick said, "Otherwise they might have second thoughts about how easy it is to kill you."

"Either that or word does not get around that my sword is called the wizard slayer," Proster said.

The king of Batend said something through the gag that neither Proster nor Garrick could understand.

"Shut up," Garrick said poking the king of Batend with his foot.

"Now what are we going to do?" Garrick asked.

"From what I could see from the tower it looked like Herwin had some help from the local residents," Proster said, "But there are three squads of orcs inside the gates. As far as I could see the orcs were not changed back just because I took out the wizard. So, we need to figure out how to change them back. Then there will not be any more killing of children."

"How do we go about finding that out?" Garrick asked, "You killed the wizard."

"By asking him," Proster pointed to the king of Batend.

"Do you think he will tell us anything?" Garrick asked.

"Let us find out," Proster said. He went over to the king of Batend. Proster took the king of Batend by the left arm. Garrick stood up and took the right arm. They dragged him to the dais and on to it then to the throne. They untied his hands, but held on to them. The king of Batend tried to get his hands to his mouth to remove the gag. Proster and Garrick pinned his arms to the arms of the chair. They tied the king of Batend's arms down. When they were finished the king of Batend fought for a few minutes before giving up. He said something through the gag.

"We are not ready for you to talk yet," Proster said. The king of Batend did not say anything else.

Proster and Garrick untied the king of Batend's feet and tied them to the leg of the chair. When they had finished that they stood a looked at their work.

"Now we are ready for you to talk," Proster told the king of Batend, "But all we are interested in is how to change the orcs back into humans. Anything else we have no interest in."

Proster took the gag out.

"You cannot..." the king of Batend started. Proster shoved the gag back in before he could finish.

"That does not sound like anything we want to hear," Proster said, "We can resort to torture if it required, but it would take up too much time and get messy. Why go there when we can do this diplomatically? All we want to know is how to change the orcs back to humans."

Proster took the gag out.

"You will never..." the king of Batend started. Proster shoved the gag back in.

"Apparently that is useless," Proster turned to Garrick, "He is not into the diplomatic stuff."

"Do we actually need him for any else?" Garrick asked, "Because if we do not then we can probably find another way to change the orcs back to humans. The wizard's spell book probably has the spell to reverse it. We just go back up there and look around. The battle outside is at a stalemate until we open the gate. We just kill him and head to the tower."

The king of Batend say something through the gag.

"Now you have something to say?" Proster asked. He removed the gag.

"You will never find a reverse spell," the king of Batend said.

"Why not?" Proster asked.

"Because there is no reverse spell," the king of Batend answered.

"I do know a thing or two about magic," Proster said, "There is always a way to reverse it."

"Not with this spell," the king of Batend smiled.

"Okay," Proster said. He punched the king of Batend before stuffing the gag back in.

"Now what?" Garrick asked.

"If there is no reverse spell and the wizard is dead, then the only other thing it could be is a charm," Proster said, "And the wizard did not have anything thing on him that could be the charm. The king, however, has several items on him that could be used for such."

The king of Batend quit smiling behind the gag. Proster smiled at him.

"I told you I know something about magic," Proster said. Then he walked to the edge of the dais and sat down. He stared at the floor just below the throne. He seemed to get lost in thought. Proster stayed like that for several minutes.

Finally, his eyes came back into focus and he looked up at the king.

"Well?" Garrick asked.

"Four of his rings are charms," Proster said, "But nothing else about him is magically."

"Four?" Garrick said, "We are only looking for one charm. Which one is the one for changing the men back?"

"We will have find out by trial and error," Proster said. He went over to the king of Batend and tried taking off rings, but the king of Batend tightened his fingers so that it was impossible to take them off without doing damage.

"You can relax them," Proster told him, "or I can I break them or cut them off." The king of Batend relaxed his fingers. Proster took off the four rings. He dropped the first one on the floor and then pulled out his sword. He broke the ring with his sword.

Nothing happened. Proster and Garrick waited several minutes before Proster dropped the next ring. He broke that one with his sword as well and again he and Garrick waited. Again nothing happened. Proster dropped the next one and used his sword to break it.

Suddenly the king of Batend changed. He had been about middle-aged with brown hair and hazel eyes. He had looked like he ate well every day. Now only his clothes were the same. His skin was now grey. He no longer had hair. His ears and chin were pointed. He was skinny.

"What is he?" Garrick asked.

"A demon of some kind," Proster answered, "Explains certain behaviours, but does not really matter. Any magically ability he had came from the wizard. I have heard that many demons without abilities will come through the portal because they cannot get very far in their realm. Here they can do all kinds of things as long as they look human."

"What do we do with him?" Garrick asked.

"Nothing yet," Proster answered.

He dropped the final ring on the floor and used his sword to break it. There was a blast from outside. It was enough to shake the castle.

Proster and Garrick waited until it had stopped.

"Did that change them back or just kill them?" Garrick asked.

"I do not know," Proster answered. He headed for the door.

"What about the thing that had been the king of Batend?" Garrick called.

"You stay and watch him," Proster called back.

Proster left the throne room. He went back down the corridor to the door at the other end. He opened it carefully and stuck his head out.

Where there had been squads of orcs waiting for the attack were now the human army recruits. Proster guessed some to be as young as thirteen. They were all lying in the court yard and none of them were moving. Proster stepped outside and went over to the closest one. He checked for a pulse. The boy was still alive. Proster straighten up and looked over the group again. This time he could see that they were breathing.

Proster went around the bodies of the boys to the gate into the city. He opened the gate a little bit. He saw that his men were waiting as well as the group of city residents. The guards had all been dealt with. Proster opened the door far enough that he could step outside. Herwin came over to him as well as another man. The other man was about middle aged, solid but not trained as a warrior. He had black hair and clothes that cost enough for him to be a merchant.

"What happened?" Herwin asked.

"Garrick and I have the king of Batend tied to his throne," Proster said, "The wizard is dead and the army that was waiting for you are back to being human. Though they have not woken up yet. The distraction worked well."

"The fight out here went well," Herwin said, "And we received unexpected help. This is Emory. He has been gathering people for a resistance against the king for a while."

"I have been working with the other people of this city to take out the evil man that is destroying our lives," Emory said, "We have been working on his downfall. Your men just sped up the process."

"Thank you for your help," Proster said.

Emory opened his mouth to say more.

"There are still some things we need to sort out," Proster turned back to Herwin, "If you and Emory come with me, we will go talk to Garrick, who is still in the throne guarding the king of Batend."

Emory turned and signalled for his group to wait. Then he and Herwin followed Proster back into the court yard. They went around the bodies and into the castle. The corridor was still empty as they went through it to the throne room.

In the throne room Garrick was still standing beside the king of Batend, who was still tied to his throne and gagged.

"What is that?" Emory asked pointing to the king of Batend.

"Your demon king," Proster said. Proster, Herwin and Emory went over and up on the dais.

"Why have you not killed it?" Emory asked pulling out his sword.

"Because I have a better idea," Proster said. He took Emory's sword away from him.

"I would rather you did not screw up my plans," Proster said.

"What now?" Herwin asked, "We have the king, the army is back to normal and we hold the capital."

"I need a group to help me escort the king of Batend to his punishment," Proster said, "Once we find him new clothes. While I am doing that the men should clean up the rest of the castle and make sure there is no one left that is likely to attack us."

"I will lead the cleaning up of the castle," Garrick said, "That will give me an idea of what we have for supplies."

"I will go gather men to go with you," Herwin said, "Vila, Loic and Menawa are probably still waiting to find out whether we won or not."

Herwin and Garrick headed out of the throne room.

"It would be best if you and your men went back to your jobs," Proster told Emory.

"I want to go with you to wherever you are taking this thing for punishment," Emory said pointing at the king of Batend.

"You can, but the rest of your men need to get back to their jobs," Proster said.

"I will go talk to them," Emory said. He left the throne room.

The king of Batend said something through the gag.

"You can shut up," Proster told him.

Three hours later Proster, Herwin, Emory, and three more of Proster's men were riding away from the capital city with the king of Batend riding with them. Proster had found some rags for the king of Batend to wear before burning the clothes that he had been wearing. Emory had talked his men into going back to work, though Proster suspected that Emory suggested to his men that there might be more fighting later. Garrick and the rest of

Proster's men were busy going through the castle. And most of the rest of the residents of the capital city looked up briefly as Proster's party rode passed them, but then went back to work.

Proster led his party along the road for a while before turning into the forest. He went deeper and deeper into the forest. When it got too hard for the horses to get through Proster had the group walk. The king of Batend tried to escape a few times, but with both his hands and feet tied he did not get very far on any of his attempts.

Finally to the relief of the whole group they came to a clearing. Only once in the clearing did they see the portal. It was about eight feet high, five feet wide and appeared to have to depth to it. It was just swirling silver and blue.

"What is that?" Emory asked.

"It is a portal," Proster answered, "It is how magic entered our world. It is also how the king of Batend entered our world."

"How do you close it?" Emory asked.

"I do not know," Proster answered, "No one has ever been able to figure that out. However, every few beings can cross from that side without some kind of assistance from this side."

"So, you are just going to send that thing home?" Emory asked, "With no guarantee that he will not come back."

"I doubt he will come back," Proster said, "Most portals have guardians that prevent that type of thing."

"How?" Emory asked.

"I do not know how they work," Proster answered, "I know something about portals, but I am not an expert on them."

Proster went over to the king of Batend. He took a bottle out of his pouch and sprinkled some of the water from it on to the king of Batend. Then he signalled his men. Two of his men picked up the king of Batend and tossed him into the portal. He disappeared into the swirling silver and blue. Then he was gone.

"Now back to the city," Proster said. He and the men left the clearing. Emory followed.

When they reached the capital city Emory left the party after they entered the city gates. Proster and the rest of this party headed up to the castle.

Inside the castle Proster and his men found Garrick and some others in the throne room. They had brought in a table and a couple chairs.

"Did it go well?" Garrick asked.

"The king of Batend will never be returning to Batend," Proster answered, "What have you found?"

"We found a map of the castle and one of the kingdom in the study," Garrick answered, "We have been in every room, except the tower. I have an inventory right here." Garrick pointed to one of the three scrolls of parchment that were on the table. The other two appeared to be the maps mentioned before.

"Summarize it for me," Proster requested as he sat down in one of the chairs.

"The study appears to be untouched," Garrick said, "Most of the furniture has been removed, as well as the decorations. In fact the only things he appeared to keep around was food. Anything else is lacking. The servants have said they that they have worked here before he took over and have been kept around for the human guards.

Even then the number of servants is not enough to keep up the castle."

"Anyone in the dungeon?" Proster asked.

"No," Garrick answered, "It looked like where the orcs slept when they were not given anything else to do. It stinks like it anyway."

"Where is everyone?" Herwin asked.

"Some are still exploring," Garrick answered, "Some have started into a barrel of wine that was brought up from the cellar, and the rest are around somewhere."

"As long as they are not bothering the city residents, I do not care what they do," Proster said, "After all what is the point of conquering if there is no celebrating."

"What do you need us to do now?" Herwin asked.

"Stay in within the castle gates," Proster answered, "Otherwise, you might want to find where you want to sleep and I heard there is enough food to go around."

"And still last you through the winter," Garrick said.

"Go celebrate," Proster said. All of the men started for the door. Proster stayed seated. At the door Herwin and Garrick stopped and looked back.

"Do you need anything?" Garrick asked.

"Not at the moment," Proster answered, "when I do I will go find it."

"Okay," Garrick said. He and Herwin left the throne room.

Proster sat there until he could not hear voices or footsteps anymore. Proster unrolled the map of the kingdom all the way and anchored down the edges. It was twice the size of Grackle. The map showed where the original country was broken up in pieces for lords. Proster counted them. There were about fifty five in total.

Which might work well, or it might not. Proster studied the map for a long time. He looked at which countries it neighboured and went over in his head what he knew about those countries. He went over where the various villages were and where the estates were.

Finally, Proster rolled the map back up and unrolled the other one. He studied it long enough to know where the kitchens were. Then he got up and left the throne room. Going through the hallways he found his way to the kitchen. Based on what he saw on his way there he would say that his men were well and thoroughly into celebrating their victory. Proster had not seen many of the servants, but he expected that they were either in hiding or had taken the day off.

The kitchen had several men gathered around the table eating and drinking while playing a dice game. The cooks had joined the game and leaving any of the cooking to whomever felt like it. There was plenty of food sitting out that was already cooked. Proster took some of what was already prepared and a goblet of wine. He sat down on a stool and set his plate and glass down on a clean area of the counter.

The game continued as if he was not even there, which was fine with him. He did not like gambling with his men. And it had nothing to do with the royal versus common thing. It was losing versus winning. He had never been any good at dice in his entire life. He had a good teacher and plenty of practice against said teacher as well as a few other people. Luck was a fickle master and Proster was never very good a being a servant. In a fight he was good, dealing with men he could handle without a problem, but gambling was the fastest way for him to lose money aside from throwing it into a fire. And Proster did not want his men to know. The teacher and former players were long ago and back before he started gathering men and they could not tell anyone. With no one to tell people his weakness, Proster found it safe as it was. His men used to invite him to play, but he always declined. Now they did not even bother to invite him. Proster did not mind. If they did not invite him, he did not have decline, and no one was likely to ask why he did not play. That worked for him.

Proster finished his food. He placed his dishes in the sink before leaving the kitchen. He headed to the junction of the four corridors. Having studied the map he now could find it without too much difficulty. He found more of his men in various states of drunkenness. He even found Garrick and Herwin sitting at a table that had been scavenged from somewhere. They had a bottle of something and were challenging each other and the other two men at the table to drinking the liquor out of the bottle. They were all so drunk that they did not even notice when Proster stopped briefly to watch them.

Proster found the junction and went down the corridor that would take him to the study and the wizard's tower. Getting to the end of the corridor, he looked into the study. Aside from the disturbed dust and a couple papers that had been moved it looked like everything had been left as it was. Proster left the study alone and went up the stairs to the tower. For the second time that day Proster went up the spiral staircase to the tower. The door at the top was closed, just as he had left it. Proster opened the door and went inside. The wizard's body was still lying in the middle of the room. The fire had gone out as there was not much for fuel where it had been lit and the wizard was not there to keep the spell going. There was more blood around the body. But other than those two things it looked exactly the same as when Proster left. Proster pulled out his sword before he stepped inside the room. Some spells disappeared after a wizard died and some continued for a long time after.

Proster stepped over the body to study what was on the shelves. There was very little of interest. He went over and looked at what was on the table. Again there was very little of interest. He found a curtain hiding a door. He pulled the curtain to one side and opened the door. Inside was a small room with no windows, only one ever burning torch, a bed with a few blankets, and enough security spells that Proster could taste them. Proster closed the door. There was nothing of interest in the wizard's tower. Proster stepped back over the body on his way out. He closed the door behind him. But this time he put the bar in place over the door. On the bar he traced a rune with his sword. This would stop people from being able to get inside the wizard's tower and prevent anyone from getting into magical trouble. Proster went back down the spiral staircase.

At the bottom he went into the study. This time he sat down at the desk. He started going through the papers that were there. Most of them had to do with the everyday activities of running a kingdom. Some were random bits of paper that had been notes of the last king to use the study. Near the bottom of the stack Proster found a family tree. It looked to be the family tree of the kings of Batend. There were several notes on the side of the page. Whoever had been here before the demon had kept this information up to date. It listed each family member and each one that actually spent time in power. It looked like it might have been bigger if each ruler had more than one heir. For ten generations each couple had one child and that child married and had one child. Except for the last name on the list, that couple had no children. However there was a note saying that the woman had lost a child and had not been able to conceive again. Based on the dates next to the names Proster figured that the man would have been about the age as the disguise that the demon wore. Proster wondered if the demon took over the king's physical appearance and then killed him and his wife. No one else must have realized what happened until the demon created his army of orcs.

Proster got up from the desk chair and went over to the hearth. It looked like the fireplace had been readied for a fire, but it had never been lit. Proster lit the fire. The flame quickly caught the dry wood. Proster went back to the desk. He gathered up all the information about the previous royal family as well as the random bits of paper. Then he threw them into the fire. Within a second they were all ashes. Proster went back to the desk. He carefully stacked the papers he thought he would need to one side of the desk. Everything else he threw into the fire.

When he was finished with the desk he started going through the shelves. General history books, philosophy books, books of fables, and that such he left on the shelves. He even put the ones that were similar on one shelf. Anything that had to do with the history of the country or the history of the royal line, Proster pulled off the shelf. He ripped the pages out and threw it piece by piece into the fire. Overall, he burned about ten books.

When the study was cleaned up, Proster sat down at the desk with a book of blank pages and a quill with a pot of ink. He opened the book to the first page before dipping the quill into the ink. Then he started writing.

The generation of the defeat of the Batend army. Prince Proster of Grankle of removed the king from his throne and renamed the country Proster. Within the next month Proster will finish taking the rest of the country. King Thedious of Grackle is expected to arrive within two weeks. He will find that Proster will not turn control over to him.

Proster wrote out a whole page before putting the quill to one side. He got up from the chair. Proster picked up one of the chairs from in front of the desk. He moved it to closer to the fire place. He sat down in the chair and stared into the fire to think. He had been sitting there for less than five minutes when his head dropped to his chest and he fell asleep.

PROSTER TAKES OVER BATEND AND KING THEDIOUS VISITS HIM

Proster sat down in the throne that had been dragged over to the table for him. Herwin and Garrick were already seated. Emory was sitting on a chair that had been brought in for him. It looked like it had been brought from the kitchen.

The four of them were gathered around the table in the throne room. The map of the country was laid out on the table top.

Three days ago Proster and his men had taken over the castle. Some of the men were still recovering from the victory celebrations. There were enough sober and ready that when the group of guards showed up with the shipment from the harvest in one of the small towns that the guards were arrested and the shipment confiscated. Then Emory had shown up demanding to know what was going to happen to the capital city and the kingdom. He sounded like if someone else did not take charge soon he would, which was why they were all now gathered around the table in the throne room.

Now that Proster was seated everyone turned to him.

"I keep being asked what is going to happen," Emory said, "But I have not been able to answer that question. They want answers to the state of their country."

"We have not discussed what is going to happen," Proster said, "Because of that I have not sent anyone to inform you to any changes."

"Then perhaps it is time to discuss these things," Emory said.

"However, I have been thinking about it," Proster said.

"How about letting us in on those thoughts," Emory said.

"My thoughts were that I would take over as king and I would give each of these holdings to my men," Proster replied, "The rest of my men would then make up the army."

Emory did not look happy about Proster's thoughts, but he did not immediately say anything.

"That sounds good," Garrick said.

"My group helped with the takeover of the city," Emory said, "You cannot dismiss what we did."

"Actually, we can," Herwin replied, "The frontal assault was a distraction and the men that were part of the attack could have handled things without your help."

"My group-" Emory started.

"But those thoughts are just that, thoughts," Proster interrupted Emory, "They are not necessarily what is going to happen. Since you are here, I was hoping that you could answer some of my questions."

"You can ask" Emory said, "but I was never a member of the king's circle of advisors."

"This map is divided up into holdings as if at one point there were lords," Proster said, "but I have not seen anything about any current lords. What happened to them?"

"The king before the one you took out dismissed them from their positions," Emory answered, "My father was a lord, but then the king decided that lords were an unwarranted expense. He kicked them out and took all their possessions. Then he removed them from public record. All of them become regular citizens, except that most did not have any money to start them off. Most died the first winter or ended up begging on the streets. A few, like my father, became tradesmen and built themselves a life. There are about three families left. The lords themselves are all died. All the money and land now belong to the throne. For a little while it looked like the king might give back some of the land, but he must have changed his mind. Or he was just using the suggestion to keep us from outright attacking him."

"The original king might have been thinking about it," Proster said, "The demon must have killed the original king and then taken his place. What happened to the queen?"

"I did not know," Emory answered, "She just disappeared. There were rumours that she was pregnant again and was bedridden, but she never reappeared. About that time news from the castle diminished to just about nothing. The guards became meaner and the servants refused to gossip. After that the king started coming up with his new policies that made life miserable."

"How long ago was that?" Proster asked.

"Six years, approximately," Emory answered.

"If there is money around here," Garrick said, "where is it? We did not find any when we went through the castle."

"I do not know," Emory said, "I know that there should be a lot of money. The king wanted money and food."

"Food, it is not necessary to hide," Proster said, "but with the servants and guards he would want to hide the money. He would do what he thought he had to protect it."

"What about getting the wizard to protect it?" Herwin asked.

"The wizard was human," Proster answered, "The king would hide it somewhere that he thought was safe from the wizard. That and the wizard's tower is not that big."

"We will have to search the castle more thoroughly," Garrick said.

"Later," Proster said, "right now we need to make some decisions. Emory, do you know which holding was your father's?"

"He kept a record," Emory answered, "it was this one." Emory pointed to one of the holdings to the south of the area of the map. It was one of the smaller holdings.

"Do you know where the holdings are of the other two families?" Proster asked.

"Brenton's father told him that this was the family's holding," Emory pointed to holding close to the capital city, "And Hervay does not know exactly where his family's holding is, but that it was in the east."

"That leaves fifty two holdings and ninety four men," Herwin sad.

"I was aware of that difficulty before any of the rest of this came up," Proster said, "It might be best if each man chose whether they wish to remain in the army or whether they want some land. There are other occupations if they did not want to do either. We will discuss that with the men later."

"Does that mean that I can take back my family's holding?" Emory asked.

"Under specific conditions," Proster answered.

"What are those conditions?" Emory asked.

"The first is that you will have to use your own money for things," Proster said, "I promised my men wealth and glory. That means I need the money to pay them as well as refinish the castle."

"That is fine," Emory said, "anything else?"

"Yes," Proster answered, "you can keep any records that relate to your personal family history, but I want you to destroy any history of the kingdom. I will be renaming the kingdom. I want to start fresh and any history will get in the way."

"If I refuse?" Emory asked, "History is very important to my family."

"As I said you can keep any family history," Proster said, "as long as the name Batend is gone from the records and any history of the kingdom in general is gone. If you are not willing to do so then you will not be given your family holdings back. I have men who can take that holding. And I am not beyond killing people that get in my way. You have worked too hard to get your family's belongings back to waste it all on this one point."

"I do not like it," Emory said, "History is a very valuable thing."

"I am not disputing that," Proster said, "nor am I saying that you have to destroy all history, just anything of Batend in general and wipe out the name from the rest of it."

"Fine," Emory said, "would you like me to take those conditions back to Brenton and Hervay?"

"If you could," Proster said, "while you are at it you can take the news that there will be an announcement tomorrow as to what will happen to the kingdom. All the people's questions will be answered."

"Okay," Emory said. He got up and left the throne room.

"What now?" Herwin asked.

"Collect as many of the men that you can," Proster answered, "Sober and awake are preferred. They are going to help us search this castle for gold."

"Okay," Herwin said. He and Garrick started to stand.

"The only place no one is allowed is the wizard's tower," Proster said.

"We will let them know," Garrick said. Garrick and Herwin started for the door to the throne room. Proster studied the map of the castle for a few more minutes before getting up and following them out.

They gathered up fifty men that were able to help with the search. The men were given the instructions and then they broke into smaller groups to go off and search. Each group had been given a section to start in.

Proster with two other men started with the throne room. They found the door that was behind the dais that led to the study and they found a trap door in the floor of the throne room that opened to a set of stairs. Following the stairs down, the group found they led to the dungeon. There was nothing else in the throne room. Even the dais had nothing to hide. The group moved to searching the staircase that led from the throne room to the dungeon.

They finished that and did not find anything. So they moved on to the rest of the dungeon. The smell down here was pretty bad as it had obviously been used to house the orcs, it also made for some awful searching because no one had cleaned it out yet. There was another search group already down there. In order to shorten their time in the fumes they joined together in searching.

When two groups finished and were headed back up the ground floor of the casdtle, Vila came down the stairs towards them.

"Proster," Vila called.

"What?" Proster asked.

"Garrick said that I should come and get you," Vila said, "we found something on the second floor."

"I am coming," Proster said. Vila turned around and starting going back up the stairs. Proster followed him. The group that had been searching with Proster went with him and the other group that had been searching the dungeon continued their search.

On the second floor, Proster found six men, including Garrick, standing outside an opened door. Most of the doors in this corridor were bedrooms. Though Proster could see into the rooms and most of them were without furniture. When Proster reached the room everyone stepped out of the way to let him get to the doorway. Proster looked into the room. This room was decorated to be fit for a queen. There was even a door that opened up into the dressing room. The bed was fancy and all the rest of the furniture was still there in good condition. It looked like with a little dusting it could be livable in a short amount of time except for the two bodies lying on the bed. They looked like they had been there for six years and were little more than skeletons with clothes. Both were in their night clothes and based on those clothes Proster guessed that the couple on the bed were the king and queen.

"Well, we now know what he did with the original king," Proster commented as he stepped into the room. He looked around.

"There is no blood on the clothes," Garrick said following him into the room.

"But there is fingernail marks on the door," Proster said pointing to the back of the door, "They tried to get out. When that did not work they just lied down and let the end come."

"I doubt it was that easy," Garrick said.

"They did not die from dehydration," Proster pointed to the glass on the table near the bed. There were marks on the side of the glass to show where the water had been before it had dried up completely.

"Probably poisoned themselves when they realized that they were no getting out," Garrick said, "A cowardly way to go."

"I do not think it was just hopelessness that had them drinking poison," Proster said, "With the way they are lying together, I would say that they wanted to died together rather than watching each other starve to death."

"I cannot see loving someone so much that you would poison yourself to die with them," Garrick said.

"Lock up the room for now," Proster said, "We will bury them later."

"Yes, sir," Garrick said. Proster left the room and Garrick followed him out. Garrick locked the door behind them. Proster led his group back down to the main floor. The other groups continued on to the next rooms in the corridor.

Down on the main floor, Proster and his group were just about to continue their searching when Mati came down the corridor.

"We found it," Mati yelled when he saw them, "We found where he was hiding the gold." Mati stopped and gestured for them to coming with him. As soon as Proster and group started in his direction he headed back the way he had come.

They followed him all the way to the kitchen and then though the kitchen to the storerooms beyond it. There were several that were filled with an assortment of foods. The last store room was filled with wine, in bottles and barrels. Mati went passed all of these to the back of the store room, where Tupac was waiting for them. Where there should have been the back wall there was a false wall that was open to reveal gold glittering in the torch light.

Proster went passed Mati and Tupac and into the room. It was about twice the size of the storeroom and it was filled with gold. If Proster could not see the back wall over the top of the pile he would not have known how large the room was. It was a lot of gold.

"This was the only store room with a false wall," Mati said.

"You think there is more gold around somewhere?" Proster asked.

"The wall has not been moved in several months at least," Mati said, "There was too much dust to have it been moved sooner. I doubt that he would not move it in that long unless he was hiding gold somewhere else as well."

"Which means he could have several hiding spots," Proster said.

"You did promise wealth," Tupac said.

"I did," Proster said, "but I did not think it would be quite so much. Each of us will be independently wealthy and still be able to run a kingdom. Let us keep searching." Proster stepped back into the store room. Tupac closed the false wall. All of them left the store room. Mati and Tupac continued their search of the area while Proster and his group went back to where they had been searching.

By the supper time they had found three other stashes of gold in the castle all about the same size as the first one and one that was half that size. The news had quickly spread to the rest of the men. That night the cooks served supper in the dining hall. Everyone sat at the long table to eat. All the men were there tonight. Some had been up most of the day and some had just gotten up, but they were all there. The some of the servants had turned up and they were serving the meal. Proster had talked to as many of the servants that he could find. When he asked he found that about three quarters of them had returned and the rest were not expected to come back unless they were forced back. These ones that were there were willing to keep working at the castle and doing their jobs. They did not care who was sitting on the throne.

The meal finished and the men continued to sit in the dining hall. They knew that Proster would address them tonight. Proster had gotten into a conversation with the castle steward and had missed most of the meal, so while the rest of the men were finished eating he was still eating on his food. No one was going to interrupt him, even if they were impatient to hear what he had to say. They sat and drank while they waited. During the meal they had ale, but now they all wanted to be sober for Proster's announcement so they were drinking water.

Finally Proster finished eating and had his plate taken away by one of the servants. He pushed back his chair and stood up.

"We defeated the king of Batend," Proster said, "We are victorious." He paused while the men cheered.

"We defeated the wizard and brought down the army," Proster said. His men cheered.

"The kingdom is now ours," Proster shouted. The cheering and applause went on for several minutes. Proster waited for them to quiet down before he continued.

"Not only that, but we have enough gold to last us three life times or more," Proster said, "We have our wealth and our glory. We have everything we have been seeking." His men cheered. Proster clapped and cheered along with them. The amount of noise they made was probably enough to be heard outside the castle.

It was several minutes before the group quieted down.

"Before we go any farther," Proster said when the group was quiet again, "I would like to take a minute for silence in remembrance of those who gained glory, but did not live to see the wealth." Proster bowed his head.

The group was silent as many of the men did the same. There were ninety five men in that dining hall and it was silent. A mouse sneezing would have echoed.

After a minute a silence the men lifted their heads. Proster lifted his head up as well, but remained quiet for a minute longer.

"We will remember them as we move on with our lives," Proster said finally, "and that is what I need to speak with you about. I plan to take the position of king of this country. Each of you will receive equal amounts of gold for your part, but there are only fifty two holdings and thus I only need fifty two lords. I hope that some of you will remain in the army as I have to rebuild the military of the kingdom. The rest have a choice. You can settle here in whatever trade you want, or you can go back to Grackle and settle there. It is your choice as to which you do, but I do need fifty two lords. Please let me know which choice you pick before tomorrow. If you wish to become a lord I will show you which is your holding. If you choose to become a lord, I ask that you visit your holding within a week, so that you can check the property and visit the people. I want people to know that they have a new king." Proster stopped and let the men absorb what he had just told them. After a few minutes there was a buzz of conversations starting.

Proster continued to stand there. The conversations grew a little louder and stayed at that volume for several minutes before dying down again.

"I am honoured to have served with all of you for so long," Proster raised his goblet, "Each of you have proven your worth in battle. You all deserve the wealth and glory gained by this venture and more. Each of you deserve to live the rest of your lives in luxury. To victory. To Wealth and Glory."

"To wealth and glory," the men replied in unison. They drank from their glasses and then Proster sat back down. The men went back to talking among themselves. Proster finished his drink and waited for them to be busy before leaving the dining hall. He went back to the throne room. Everything was as it was left earlier. Proster went to the table. There was a pot of ink and a quill that he had brought from the study. He had marked where the treasure stores were on the map of the castle. This time he unrolled the map of the country. He opened the ink and dipped the quill into it. Proster crossed out Batend on the map and wrote in Proster.

"King Proster of Proster," Proster muttered to himself, "That sounds nice." He put the quill to one side and waited.

The wait was not very long. The first man arrived to tell Proster of his choice. It was Loic and he wished to stay in the army. Proster made note of that on another piece of parchment he had brought from the study. Loic left the throne and passed another man on his way in.

Slowly over the course of the evening each of Proster's men came in and told him what they wish to do with their lives. If they wanted to be lords, Proster showed them their holdings. If they wanted to stay in his army, he made a note of that. If they wanted to settle down, Proster shook their hand and wished them well. Proster did note that those who chose to settle down none of them wanted to return to Grackle.

Finally Proster had fifty lords, thirty members to his army and fourteen men leaving his service. That was when Herwin and Garrick came through the door way and into the throne room. They each sat down in a chair at the table.

"Everyone stated what they want?" Herwin asked.

"I missing two," Proster replied, "And I am short two lords. Would either of you like those positions?"

"If you are going to be king then you are going to need some advisors," Garrick said, "And that has been our job for several years. But if you want us to be lords than we need to go visit our holdings regularly, that might be a problem."

"Not really," Proster said, "I have two holdings left, and both are within riding distance of the castle." Proster pointed them out to Herwin and Garrick.

"I know that you both are my advisors," Proster said, "I also know that you do not want to give up that power, so I arranged that you can get here in the shortest amount of time possible. I know you would argue otherwise, but I am making you both lords because as much as you are my advisors you need to have your own lives."

"I will go out to my holding after the announcement tomorrow," Garrick said, "And be back with in two days."

"At which point I will go," Herwin said.

"Anything else you need?" Proster asked when neither of them moved.

"We want to know why you are into destroying history and renaming the country after yourself," Herwin answered.

"I could not think up a better name for the country," Proster said.

"And the destroying the history?" Herwin asked.

"I do not want to live in the past," Proster answered, "I want to start new and I think it would be a good idea if the country starts new as well."

"It still sounds like an ego trip," Herwin said.

"I asked each of the brand new lords what their holdings are now called," Proster said, "Aside from the five unnamed ones, the majority chose their own name for the holding. It might be an ego trip, but it is a popular one." Herwin and Garrick studied the map of the country for several minutes.

"Is this one Herwin or this one?" Herwin asked pointing to the two holdings without names.

"That one," Proster pointed to the one that was east of the capital city. Proster wrote the name in before turning to Garrick.

"I will name mine after I have seen what it looks like," Garrick said, "I do not believe we need a holding named after me."

"As stated that choice is up to you," Proster said. Herwin and Garrick stood up and left the throne room. Proster closed the pot of ink. He left the map unrolled as he got up. He went through the door behind the throne and into the study.

The servants had started the fire in the fireplace. Proster sat down in the chair where he had been sleeping for the last several days. He let the heat from the fire warm him. Only once he left comfortably warm did he fall asleep.

Proster walked out on to the balcony that faced the court yard, which was full of the people of the capital city. They were packed in tightly and Proster knew that there were more outside the wall. Proster looked over the crowd. The last time he had been in front of a crowd this big was for the ceremony where King Thedious named Alaric his heir. Yet, he found that he was not nervous. He figured that it must be something to do with royal blood.

"Good citizens," Proster projected his voice, "four days ago we entered your city with the intention of removing your king. Now, we stand victorious in our objective. You may have noticed that many that were taken into the army have returned to you. That is only the first of several policy changes I am going to make as your new king."

There was no thunderous applause, or noises of discontent. The people were waiting for good news or bad news that might affect them.

"From now on the only people that will being joining the army are those who wish to choose that as their career path. The second policy change I need to tell you about it that I am asking that you not send me everything you make or grow. I wish only ten percent of your profits for taxes. This is not to provide for me, but to create and sustain programs that will benefit you. As yet I do not know what these programs will be."

There was a little bit of applause. Anything that meant more money in their pocket was a good thing, but Proster knew they would rather that he used the money that had already been taken from them to fund any programs. Then there would be no tax, and when the money ran out they would revolt at the idea of being taxed to provide them with the programs. It would be easier just to knock the tax down to ten percent and not have to deal with rebellion later. It was better than what they were paying.

"My men have been given titles and holdings through the country," Proster said, "This is to help me run the country. If you live in an area under their rule you must pay their taxes as well."

This was met with silence, but Proster did not expect them to applaud that.

"And one other change," Proster said, "the last thing of which I have to announce. I have renamed the country. This country is no longer Batend, it is Proster. And it will continue to be such from this day forward. Thank you for listening, good citizens." Proster waved before going back inside. No applause to followed him, but Proster was not expecting any. Now they would all go home and discuss his announcement and what it meant to them. There would be some discussion about what to do with this king, but no one would do anything because he promised them programs to benefit them and a lower tax rate. That would be enough to pacify people.

Now he had to split up the gold into ninety seven shares. Then he had to take one share and use it put the castle back to liveable shape. That would take a while. When he was finished with that he would have to get the kingdom back in proper running order. There were some policy changes he would need to make and an army to rebuild. All of which would take most of his attention. He would not have time to be bored when he had a kingdom to run. Not to mention that there was no other kingdom that he could invade if he did get bored. It was unlikely that anyone was going to attack him, but there might be one king that thought Proster would be easy to push over. One attempt would make the rest of them come running with peace treaties. Turning those down might be fun. Proster smiled as he headed for the throne room, where his men had been gathering the gold all together.

Proster stared at the pieces of parchment that littered his desk. It was depressing to think that all these people were willing to help put the castle back together, but none of them were willing to do it to his way or on his schedule. After the division of loot most of his men had left for their holdings. The ones that were going to settle down had taken the time to find houses and jobs before leaving. The ones that were staying in the army had started with cleaning out the barracks. Proster has used the week since then to go through every room in the castle, with the exception of the tower, and clean it up. He also figured out what he wanted in each room and wrote it down. Now he was trying to find tradesmen who were willing to do the job he wanted. He figured that he could probably hire a dozen all at once and have them working in different parts of the castle all at once, but first he had to find ones that would do what he wanted, on the schedule he wanted, and within the budget he had laid out. He did not think it would be this difficult.

A knock came at the door to the corridor.

"Come in," Proster called. The door opened and Herwin stepped inside.

"Proster," Herwin said, "Word from the front gate has reached us. King Thedious of Grackle is coming through the city toward the castle. He is probably looking for his share."

"I will see him in the throne room when he arrives," Proster said, "make certain there is an 'honour' guard in the throne room so that if necessary he and whoever is with him can be thrown out of the castle."

"Yes, sir," Herwin said. He left the study and closed the door behind him. Proster looked at the pieces of parchment again. That situation did not seem any better than it was before, but it did seem better than the alternative. Proster gathered up all the pieces of parchment. He shuffled them into a pile and then tossed them into the fire. Such estimates seemed to be pointless and a waste of a large amount of paper. He would find a better way to pick who would do the work.

From the throne room Proster could hear the sounds of people moving around, but he could not hear his father's voice so he knew his father had not arrived. Proster adjusted his clothes and smoothed down his hair before opening the door that led to the throne room. He found the guards already in their positions. He closed the door behind him and let the curtain drop into place. Proster stepped up on the dais and sat down in the throne. The guards must have moved the throne because Proster remembered moving it back to the table to discuss some things with Herwin and Garrick the evening before. The table was still sitting there with the maps as well as some other papers that had wandered to it. Proster slumped down in the chair and placed his elbow on the arm rest. He put his chin into his palm. He lowered his eye lids to half way and put a bored expression on his face. The moment he had finished posing himself, the door opened and Herwin stepped inside the throne room.

"King Thedious of Grackle," Herwin announced.

"He is my son, he knows who I am," King Thedious told Herwin as he stepped into the throne room. Several servants followed him, but he had no guards with him. Proster was not expecting him to have any because that would mean that he had started his own army. King Thedious started up the red carpet toward the throne. He was just about to step on to the dais when Loic stepped in front of him.

"No one may approach King Proster without his permission," Loic told King Thedious, "you must stay off the dais."

"What are you talking about?" King Thedious asked, "He is my son."

"You still need permission to go any closer to him," Loic said.

"What is he going on about?" King Thedious demanded of Proster as he looked around Loic.

"It is as he said," Proster answered in a bored tone of voice, "This is my throne room and here I am king. That means that you need my permission to come any closer. You do not have my permission, family or not."

"You are my son," King Thedious's voice was threatening, "I came for my share."

"Your share of what?" Proster asked.

"You and your men are under my command as the king of Grackle," King Thedious answered, "as such you own me a percentage of what you have looted."

"No, I do not," Proster said.

"You are subjects under my rule," King Thedious said.

"You ordered me to stop my attack," Proster said, "You commanded me to turn back and go home. You demanded that I do as I was told. And you threatened me if I did not do as you said. That means that I broke your rules and your orders, as such I am no longer your subject by the laws of your kingdom. Since I am no longer your subject I get to keep everything I earned when I attacked Batend and took the capital city. You get nothing."

"Proster," King Thedious started.

"King Proster!" Proster interrupted him, "You are in Proster now and I am king of this country. You would not feed my men or my animals when I was your subject. You forced me to find some way for feeding them. Now I have found a way to do that. We were Grackle`s army since I was sixteen and never once did you appreciate us. Now we are appreciated and no one can tell us to do or not do anything. You lost your control and you will never get it back."

King Thedious opened his mouth to say something, but by the look on his face he was going to say something in anger.

"Loic, escort King Thedious out of my throne room," Proster said, "he has worn out his welcome."

"Yes, sire," Loic said, "Would you like me to escort them outside the castle gate or all the way out of the city?"

"Outside the city is good," Proster said.

"Yes, sire," Loic said. The guards each took hold of King Thedious's servants. Loic and Tupac each took an arm of King Thedious and the group left the throne room. King Thedious fought to stay, but he was no match for Loic and Tupac.

Finally the only ones left in the throne room were Proster and Herwin.

"He is not happy," Herwin said.

"That is what he gets for coming here and expecting his share," Proster stood up.

"Proster," Herwin said as Proster started forward and off the dais.

"Yes," Proster said.

"I will be leaving tomorrow and I will be gone for several weeks," Herwin said, "Garrick sent word that he would not be back here for another couple days."

"That is fine," Proster said, "I can handle things for a couple days. The only decisions I am likely to make are redecorating the castle."

"Did you figure out which tradesmen to hire?" Herwin asked.

"I tossed all those pieces of paper into the fire," Proster answered, "They did not tell me anything that was useful and did not want to do as I ordered." Proster walked passed Herwin and out of the throne room. Herwin followed him and fell into step besides him.

"So, what are you going to do?" Herwin asked.

"Talk to some of the tradesmen in the city," Proster answered, "Perhaps in person I can get more information than a piece of paper will tell me."

"What happens if none of them meet your expectations even in person?" Herwin asked.

"Then I geographical expand my search," Proster answered, "if that does not work then I will have to lock a couple tradesmen in the dungeon until they agree to do things my way."

"Try not to take that step before Garrick or I have returned," Herwin said.

"I heard that Garrick has fallen heads over heels for one of the locals in his holding," Proster said, "That is why he cannot get back here. So, where are you going?"

"Grackle," Herwin answered.

"To bring the woman that you were going on about back when I was suggesting this whole venture?" Proster said. They exited the castle through the doors into the court yard. Proster headed for the centre gate. Herwin continued to keep in step with him.

"You said that you thought we should have our own lives," Herwin said.

"I do not mind you finding women to fill your lives," Proster said, "I will bet that her father will be willing to give his blessing now that you are a lord, rather than the son of a whore who looked like he was going to die young."

"I was not planning on asking him anything," Herwin said, "She is the only person that I plan to ask anything of. Her father has nothing to do with what is between us."

"If you create an international incident my father might come back," Proster said.

"So, we will get a few of the warriors together and send them to discuss it with him in slightly different terms," Herwin said.

"I thought you were supposed to talk me out of that kind of thing," Proster said.

"No one is getting between me and Misa," Herwin said, "Especially since I finally get a chance to be with her." They went out the centre gate and headed down the street.

"I doubt it would take much to intimidate my father," Proster said.

"Or you could just throw him out," Herwin said.

"He is going to spend the next three days camped outside the gates of the city," Proster said, "He will be waiting for me to come out and apologize for being disrespectful."

"Wait until he finds out that you are actually king in this country," Herwin said.

"I doubt he will get the hint," Proster said as he stopped in front of a tradesmen's shop. He opened the door and Herwin followed him inside.

Herwin left the next morning as he had planned. Proster was right. It was three days before King Thedious packed up and headed back to Grackle. Proster continued to try to find a tradesmen that were willing to do what he wanted and on his schedule.

A week later Proster was getting very annoyed at tradesmen. He had already put three of them into the dungeon who had promised they could do what he wanted and then could not produce it. Proster was in the courtyard taking his frustrations out on a practice dummy with his sword when a carriage came into the court yard through the centre gate. Proster stopped hacking at the practice dummy to watch as it stopped in front of the door to the castle. The door opened and Herwin stepped out of the carriage. He turned back and offered a hand down to someone inside. A woman accepted his hand and stepped down out of the carriage. She was looking around in wonder. She had long blonde hair that was braided back. She wore a green dress that highlighted her slim waist and full bosom. Herwin did not close the carriage door. Instead Garrick stepped out next. Proster figured that Herwin had stopped in to see Garrick on his way back to the capital. Garrick also turned back and offered his hand to a lady. The lady that stepped out this time had reddish brown hair and was wearing a baby blue dress. It was not as high of quality as the blonde woman's dress. The woman in the baby blue dress had a more solid frame, but she was not fat by any standards.

Herwin and Garrick escorted the ladies inside. Proster went back to beating on the practice dummy.

Ten minutes later Herwin and Garrick came out of the side door and over to where Proster was beating the practice dummy.

"I see you are back," Proster said.

"What is this about locking tradesmen in the dungeon?" Herwin asked.

"They lied to me about what they could do," Proster answered, "I do not like dealing with people that lie to me. I see you both had good trips."

"Pepita had never been to the capital city and she wanted to see the castle," Garrick said, "I did not think you would mind."

"I do not mind," Proster said, "How long are the four of you staying?"

"A few days," Herwin answered, "Then Misa and I are heading back to my holding."

"Pepita and I will be here for the rest of the week," Garrick answered.

"Perhaps you should both find a priest while you are here," Proster suggested, "Then you can both go back to your holdings with brides."

"That would require asking the ladies if they wish to get married here," Garrick replied, "I do not intend to push her into anything that she does not want."

"Whatever you chose," Proster said.

"How long do you intend on keeping the tradesmen locked in the dungeon?" Herwin asked.

"I do not intend to let them go," Proster said, "Those kind of liars are bad for everyone and it is better if they are locked up and not bothering other people who are honest. I would have locked up more of them just for not being able to help me, but most have not lied to me. They have been honest with me in telling me that they cannot do things in my way on my schedule. I have to have some line that states what is a good reason and what is a bad reason for these kinds of things. My biggest problem is that I still cannot find tradesmen to do what I need."

"Have you tried searching outside the geographical area as you said before I left?" Herwin asked.

"I send messengers out yesterday," Proster answered, "I do not expect to hear back from them for some weeks."

"What are you going to occupy your time with until then?" Herwin asked.

"Putting together some of the policies for the kingdom that I have been ignoring in favour of decorating," Proster said, "I have things that need to be done, I just decided to start with the castle and move on from there."

"Okay," Herwin said, "If you need us you just have to send for us."

"I am aware of that," Proster said.

Herwin and Garrick went back inside. Proster continued to beat up the practice dummy.

Two days later Proster was sitting in his office going through paperwork on his latest policy when there was a knock at the door.

"Come in," Proster called while still studying the piece of paper in front of him. The door opened and Garrick stepped inside.

"What do you need?" Proster asked.

"To speak with you," Garrick said. Proster gestured to the chair that was in front of his desk. Garrick sat down in it and waited while Proster continued to read through the piece of parchment.

Finally Proster put the piece of parchment down and looked up at Garrick.

"What is it that you need to speak with me about?" Proster asked.

"Herwin and I have been talking," Garrick said, "We have also been talking with Misa and Pepita. And we were thinking about what you said about getting married before going back to our holdings. We decided that getting married was a good idea. We would like to use the throne room for the ceremony and the dining hall for the meal afterward. It would be a double ceremony. And we think we might have found a priest that is willing to do it for us."

"Okay," Proster said, "what do you need from me?"

"Permission to use the throne room," Garrick answered, "And permission to decorate the throne room in a way that is proper for a wedding."

"Since I cannot decorate it in the way I want any time soon go ahead and decorate it for the wedding," Proster said, "A wedding is an excellent use of a throne room. Beats ruling a kingdom out of it."

"I will go tell Herwin and Pepita," Garrick said. He got to his feet and left the room. Garrick closed the door behind him on his way out. Proster went back to his policy. He had just about worked all the kinks out of it.

A week went passed as Proster went through several different policies that he had planned for the kingdom. He was sitting there trying to decide what he needed for an army and if it was possible to recruit enough people wgo would be loyal to him in a kingdom that had not decided what to do with their new king, when he heard people moving around in the throne room. Proster worked for several more minutes before finally getting up and going to the door that led to the throne room. Proster opened it and looked into the throne room. There were people all over the place. Some were on ladders, some were moving furniture. It the middle of the room was a man directing it all. The man looked to be shorter than Proster's own four foot three inch frame. But this man was skinny. He had an almost elfish look to him, but Proster knew that elves were never that short. The man had short brown hair that curled making him look young. He was wearing brightly colour clothes made of quality fabric, but the whole outfit made him look good not gaudy.

The man was shouting directions to the men that were doing the decorating. Men that were five foot eight inches were listening to this short man as if he could do them serious harm if they did not. Proster stepped out of his study and closed the door behind him. He looked around. The decorations, though white, looked great. Proster wondered if he could get them to leave them up after the wedding because it was much better than the grey stone walls that plagued him every time he had to spend time in the throne room.

Proster walked over to the short man.

"You must be King Proster," the short man said when he saw Proster. He gave a short bow.

"I am," Proster said, "who are you?"

"I am Paul," the man said, "Garrick hired me to decorate for the wedding. I know it is a few days early, but Herwin said that it would be all right."

"It is fine," Proster said, "It looks great so far."

"Just wait until I am finished," Paul said, "I have this marvellous vision of just how it will look when I am finished. It will be just short of putting the brides to shame. Fortunately, they have hired brilliant dress makers to make the dresses so that they will not be too much in shame against the stunning back drop." Paul was still gesturing and pointing to the men that were doing the work. Even without him shouting they knew what they were supposed to do and what all his signals meant.

"Do you usually decorate for weddings?" Proster asked.

"I decorate all rooms," Paul said, "That is what I do for a living. Though the last several years I have had to live in Lithimin due to the poor economic conditions here. I was home visiting family when I was introduced to Garrick. He asked if I was willing to do his wedding to Pepita and I was delighted to be able to work in my country again. With the change it rulership it sounds like I might be able to find work here again. Though it is usually sparse even in good economic conditions."

"It this wedding turns out to be just as marvelous as you claim it will then I might have some work for you," Proster said.

"That would be wonderful," Paul said.

"We will discuss it when you are finished," Proster gestured to the decorating of the throne room.

"Of course," Paul said, "It is always a good idea to see a person's work before hiring them."

"Exactly," Proster said. He went back to the door to the study and opened it. He stepped inside and then closed the door behind him.

At supper time Proster went to the dining hall. He tried to avoid eating there because there were so many people living at the castle that also ate there. Some of his men had not yet found homes for themselves yet. Then there were people that were working at the castle on various projects that were being done. The servants had been told that they were allowed to eat in the dining hall with everyone else. It was crowded some evenings.

Proster did not mind his men so much because they left him alone. It was some of the others that were the problem. A few people thought that this was a good time to bring their complaints to him. They expected him to listen and find a solution all while eating his meal. Proster preferred to eat in peace. It was better for the digestion. But he had not been able to catch a servant at the right time to get his meal delivered to his study.

This evening the dining hall was especially crowded as the men helping with decorating the throne room were also there eating. Proster found a space in the corner where he could sit out of the way of people. The spot at the head of the table had been reserved for him, but Proster knew that sitting there would have directed attention to him and not left him in peace to eat his meal. The servant that brought the meals set his down in front of him and moved on without a word. When he sat at the head of the table there would be a ceremony. The castle steward would bring his meal before sitting down in his own chair to wait being served. This time a serving girl just placed the plate on the table and move on to the next person at the table. Since he was in the back corner Proster was among the last to get his food. He did not care. Everyone around him ate and ignored him.

Supper was just about finished and many people had already left when Proster saw Paul come into the room. Paul went over where Herwin and Garrick were seated up near the head of the table. He told him something. They said something back. Paul left them alone and looked around the room. When he finally spotted Proster he came over to where Proster was sitting. Paul sat down in the chair across from Proster as if this was where he had wanted to sit all along.

"I have finished decorating the throne room," Paul said, "You can come inspect my work. It would be wonderful to get work in my home country again, but I do not expect you to do anything because I said that. After you have finished I invite you to come see."

"I will," Proster said.

"If you have any questions about it I will gladly answer them," Paul said. Then he slipped out of his chair and left the dining hall. Proster went back to his meal.

When he had finished eating, Proster stood up and left the dining hall. Herwin and Garrick were still sitting there eating, though he saw Herwin glancing at the chair at the head of the table with a worried look on his face. Proster shook his head. Herwin should know better than to expect that of him. Proster headed for the throne room.

He found the door open and Paul sitting on one of the many chairs set up for guests that would be coming to the wedding. Proster stepped into the room and looked around. There white, cream and some yellows. The walls, the furniture, the dais, and floor had all been decorated. It was tasteful, stunning and not hard on the eyes. But if it was not taken down it would look fine for everyday use as well as a wedding.

"What do you think?" Paul asked as he watched Proster look over the room.

"Very good," Proster answered, "Herwin and Garrick should be happy with it for their weddings."

"The brides have already seen it and approve," Paul said.

"That is a good start," Proster said.

"Do you have any questions?" Paul asked.

"No," Proster answered.

"What kind of work do you need done?" Paul asked.

"The whole castle needs to be redecorated," Proster answered, "And I have not been successful at finding tradesmen that can do that job in the way that I want."

"You have plans drawn up for the rooms?" Paul asked.

"Some ideas written down for the rooms," Proster answered.

"May I see them?" Paul asked, "If I know what you are looking for it is easier to figure out how to do a room."

"My notes are in my study," Proster said. He headed for the door to his study. Paul stood up and followed him. Proster opened the door and went inside. Paul followed him, but did not close the door.

"I am expecting Herwin and Garrick to come and look at my work," Paul hesitated by the door, "I want to be able to see when they arrive."

"I do not care," Proster said as he pulled the stack of papers out of his desk drawer. He offered the stack to Paul. Paul took it and sat down in the chair in front of the desk. He started to go through them. Proster sat down in his chair behind the desk and waited.

Paul went through each paper and read what was written there. Finally he was back at the first page.

"You do not have much yet, but an idea," Paul said, "but I can see the rooms in my mind. It would not be difficult to do all of this." Paul offered the pages back.

"Then you will need those," Proster said nodding to the pages, "as you go through and redecorate all the rooms in the castle."

"It will take time," Paul said looking at the papers again.

"And money," Proster said, "both will be supplied. If there is anything else you need, just tell me."

"I will need a room to work out of," Paul said.

"There are plenty in the castle," Proster said, "if there is someone else in the room you want to use they can move to another room, same goes for the room you are working in."

"I will have to go get my wife," Paul said, "I had thought that it would just be the wedding I was here for so she stayed behind. So, it may take me a week before I can get started."

"That is fine," Proster said.

"Then I will go over these ideas and see the rooms," Paul got to his feet, "I will see what there is to work with. Then when I am able to start I can do so immediately."

Proster and Paul heard Herwin and Garrick entered the throne room. Paul headed back into the throne with a look that suggested he was deep in thought about the project already. Proster watched him go before getting up and closing the door behind him. Proster went back to his desk and looked down at the policy he had been dealing with that afternoon. Rather than sit back down behind the desk Proster went over and started the fire. Once it was going he sat down in the chair beside the fireplace. When he was comfortable he closed his eyes and went to sleep.

The day of the wedding arrived and the castle was busy with people making last minute preparations. Proster spent most of the morning in his study with Herwin and Garrick. They were all dressed in the uniforms they used to wear when presenting themselves to the king. All the armour was ceremonial and likely to be a hindrance if they were actually going into battle. However, it looked good in royal halls and to people with money. All of Proster's men would be wearing such armour for today, except those who had guard duty.

Fortunately it was comfortable enough to wear for most of a day.

Proster had dragged both Herwin and Garrick into his study after Garrick came close to beating up one of the servants over a minor slight. Herwin had been hovering about the entrance keeping any eye on things that were coming and going to make sure that there was nothing that was not supposed to be there. He had been tripped over three times in the course of five minutes. There was some audible sighs when Proster took them both by the elbows and got them out of the way. Now Garrick was pacing and Herwin was playing with the ceremonial dagger that was part of the uniform. Proster sat there with the list of policies that were half completed and would need to be finished very soon.

"Sit down," Proster ordered. Garrick fell into the chair without any change in expression or worried look in his eyes.

"Put that away," Proster ordered. Herwin put away the dagger, but his hands were still looking for something to play with.

"If it were any more planned it would be a coronation," Proster said.

"You did not have one of those," Herwin said. His eyes were coming back to his surroundings.

"I do not have a crown either," Proster said, "not looking to get one either. But I do need your thoughts on some of the policies I have written up." Proster offered a stack of papers to Herwin and Garrick. Both accepted them and started to read through them. Proster left them alone to read.

His thoughts drifted to the safe he knew was behind one of the bookcases. He had found it completely by accident. It held the implements of his station. The crown, the sceptre, the signet ring, and the matching tiara for the queen. He had not told anyone about his find because he figured that they would demand a coronation. Then he would be king and they would start treating him like a king, with all the pomp and ceremony that befitted that station. He was not sure he was ready for that stuffy behaviour. So, crowns and ceremonies could wait. It was not like there was a rush.

There was a knock on the door to the corridor. Herwin and Garrick looked up from their reading.

"Yes?" Proster called.

"It is Lamont the steward," a voice answered.

"Come in," Proster called. The door opened and the castle steward stepped into the room.

"All the preparations for the wedding are finished," the castle steward said.

"Thank you," Proster said.

"There is a light lunch being served in the dining hall," the castle steward said. Herwin and Garrick started to get to their feet.

"We will have ours served in here," Proster said. Herwin and Garrick sat back down.

"Also have the some sent up to the brides," Proster said.

"I will," the castle steward said. He bowed before stepping out of the room and closing the door. Herwin and Garrick went back to reading. Proster got up and pulled out a book from the bookcase behind him. He sat back down and opened it to the page he had left off on.

Five minutes later there was a knock on the door.

"Come in," Proster called. The door opened and the castle steward stepped into the room carrying a tray with food on it. He set it down on the edge of the desk where all three men could reach it.

"Food has been sent up to the brides and their helpers," the castle steward said.

"Good," Proster said.

"Is there anything else?" the castle steward asked.

"Not right now," Proster said, "Just call us when it is time for us to go to the throne room."

"I will," the castle steward said. He left the room and closed the door behind him. Proster, Herwin and Garrick ate while they read.

Most of the tray had been picked clean when there was a knock at the door.

"Yes?" Proster called.

"It is time," the steward called back. Herwin and Garrick handed back the stacks of papers to Proster before standing up. They smoothed out their uniforms. Proster stood up and went over to the door that led to the throne room. When Herwin and Garrick were ready he opened the door. Herwin and Garrick stepped into the throne room. Proster followed them out and closed the door behind him. Herwin and Garrick took their places on the dais near where the priest was standing. Proster was shown to a seat in the second row by the usher. Proster sat back to enjoy the show.

Most of the chairs were full already and there were only a few guests still coming in. For the next five minutes the usher worked to get the guests seated. Then there did not seem to be any more guests coming in. Two minutes passed. A woman came in and went over to a harp that had been set up beside the dais. She sat down on the chair and started to play.

Both brides entered and started down the aisle toward the dais as the harp played. They went to join the future husbands. The priest started into his opening prayers and comments. He talked for fifteen minutes on marriage and the seriousness of it all. Finally when he was done he went to stand near Garrick and Pepita.

"Do you, Garrick, take this this woman, Pepita, to be your wife, according to God's holy decree; do you promise to be to her a loving and loyal husband, to cherish and keep her in sickness and in health; and forsaking all others, to be faithful only to her as long as you both shall live?"

"I do," Garrick answered.

"Do you, Pepita, take this man, Garrick, to be your husband, according to God's decree; do you promise to him a loving and loyal husband, to cherish and keep him in sickness and in health; and forsaking all others, to be faithful only to him as long as you shall live?"

"I do," Pepita answered.

The priest moved to stand near Herwin and Misa.

"Do you, Herwin, take this this woman, Misa, to be your wife, according to God's holy decree; do you promise to be to her a loving and loyal husband, to cherish and keep her in sickness and in health; and forsaking all others, to be faithful only to her as long as you both shall live?"

"I do," Herwin answered.

"Do you, Misa, take this man, Herwin, to be your husband, according to God's decree; do you promise to him a loving and loyal husband, to cherish and keep him in sickness and in health; and forsaking all others, to be faithful only to him as long as you shall live?"

"I do," Misa answered.

The priest moved back to centre.

"By the power granted to me by God, I declare you husband and wife," the priest announced. The guests applauded and the couples at the front kissed.

Then they walked back down the carpet to the door and out of the throne room with the priest leading the way. The guests stood up and followed.

Proster smiled to himself as he waited from most of the room to clear before moving. Now they would have other things to do than play mother hen to him.

KING PROSTER'S CORONATION

Two years passed within the kingdom now known as Proster. King Proster gained popularity and found many loyal servants among the people he ruled over. However, several problems arose as time went on. Some of the people treated him like a king and some still would not recognize him as their king. It was claimed that he had never been officially crowned. This created more problems as these people refused to obey any of the laws that King Proster put forward. King Proster threw a few citizens into the dungeon for such behaviour, but it was pointed out multiple times that there was a simple solution to the problem and that legally he was not king until after he had been crowned. Until he did, the laws he put forward did not have to be followed by anyone.

Proster finally agreed to have a proper coronation and be crowned King of Proster. Herwin and Garrick then proceeded to plan the event before he could change his mind about it.

On the date exactly two years after the attack on the castle, Proster woke to the sounds of trumpets outside in the court yard. He crawled out of bed as he tried to remember what was happening. His head felt like it was too heavy to lift and his stomach complained every time he moved. He put his feet on the floor and found it to be cold despite the carpeting in the room. He looked around his bedroom and found that he must have actually slept there. There were no papers on the covers or on the bedside table. There was also no signs that there had been anyone else in bed with him as any point during the night.

The trumpets sounded again outside in the court yard. Proster held his head until it stopped echoing. Then he stood up and stumbled to the window. He opened the curtain and found bright mid-morning light that made him want to crawl back into bed. He blinked against it several times before he could see anything outside. Out in the court yard there were two squads in formation and dress uniform. What they were doing was not drills, but something that looked like a ceremonial guarding of a procession. Several people were coming through the centre gates with guards around them. One looked like the priest that had conducted the marriage ceremony for Herwin and Misa and Garrick and Pepita. There did not seem to anything like a bride or decorations like a wedding, so Proster was safe there. The next person he recognized being the mayor of the capital city. After that came several lords from nearby holdings and they were all dressed up in what looked like ceremonial robes. It was all red, gold and white. It looked blinding in the morning sunshine.

Proster tried to think and figure out what was going on, but the thumping and banging in his head made it difficult. The door to Proster's room opened without any knocking first. Proster turned to look and saw Herwin and Garrick come into the room. They closed the door behind them. Proster noticed that they had some clothes that were red, gold, and white in their hands, though both were dressed in their dress uniforms.

"What is going on?" Proster asked.

"Your coronation," Garrick answered, "You agreed to it and we put it together."

"Should you not be at home with your wife?" Proster asked.

"Pepita had a baby boy last night," Garrick answered, "She understands that I have to be here. And I promised her that I would be there the rest of the week to help with whatever she needed."

Herwin took Proster's elbow and directed him to the centre of the room. Proster was still trying to get his brain working and did not resist.

"This is an important day for the kingdom," Herwin said as he helped Proster take off his night shirt, "As such we need to be here to support you."

"We were drinking last night," Proster said as a memory came through the fog, "You were just as drunk as I was." Garrick handed Proster a pair of trousers that looked made to go with the red, gold and white outfit.

"Garrick woke me a couple hours ago," Herwin replied, "I have had time to get over the hangover. We did not wake you because you would have disappeared in your study and it would have been harder to get you out of there."

"If I agreed to this, why are you two trying to trick me into doing things?" Proster finished putting on the pants so Garrick handed him the shirt.

"Because it is easier for us," Herwin answered, "Now, hurry up. Your part in the ceremony will start soon."

Once Proster had the shirt on he was handed the shoes.

"Where did you get this stuff?" Proster asked.

"Emory helped us find it," Garrick answered, "The only thing we are missing from the whole ceremony is the crown. We were hoping you might tell us where that was."

"A safe in my study behind the books on ancient philosophy," Proster answered, "along with the sceptre."

"I will go get it," Herwin said. He left the room while Garrick helped Proster put on the cape.

"I feel ridiculous," Proster said as they finished with the finally accessories.

"Then you should have come up with some way to be crowned king long before this," Garrick said, "Now come on."

Garrick went to the door and opened it. Proster followed him at a slower pace because the whole outfit was heavy. They went into the hallway and headed down to the main floor. They stopped outside the door to the throne room, which was closed today. There were two guards outside as usual, but today they were wearing dress uniforms. Proster was glad to see that their weapons were real. Garrick made sure that Proster was centered in front of the door.

"Herwin and I have been talking," Garrick said.

"Apparently," Proster said.

"We think you need to find a wife," Garrick said, "A woman that will keep you company and provide the kingdom with heirs."

"I do not need to company," Proster said.

"The occasional tryst with a serving girl is not going to get you an heir," Garrick said.

"Do not tell them that," Proster said, "they seem to think that if they become pregnant that I will be forced to marry them and then they will become queen."

"I hope you have not been encouraging this rumour," Garrick said.

"I do not encourage any rumours," Proster said, "I just live with the benefits." Before Garrick could respond the doors to the throne room started to open. Garrick moved out of the way so that he would not be seen by the people inside. Once the doors were all the way open Proster could see inside. It had been set up similar to how it was for the wedding, except that people were standing not sitting in rows. Proster started forward along the carpet to where the priest was standing on the dais. When he started so did the music. Which was loud and annoying. Proster gritted his teeth to avoid giving away how much pain he was in. His steps were slow due to the weight of the clothing. Every one turned to face Proster to watch him as he went passed. If Proster was not so hung over he might have been nervous, or very angry. He was not sure which. But he thought he might have to get revenge on Herwin and Garrick at some point.

The dais was much closer to the doors into the throne room than Proster remembered because he did not have time to think up even one idea for revenge before he had reached the dais. He stepped up on it and was now standing before the priest. The priest signalled Proster to go down on his knees. Proster did so carefully due to the clothing hampering his movements.

"Proster," the priest addressed him in a formal sounding voice. It seemed to vibrate in Proster's head.

"In God's eyes everyone is equal," the priest said, "he does not see one man as better than another. He loves all equally and without bias. God does see that a king is necessary to keep his people safe and cared for. He grants this station to individuals that show qualities that are necessary to do those things for his people. I am asking for your oath in accepting this position and willingness to lead these people."

The priest paused as if he was expecting Proster to stop him and say that this was no or could he please bow out gracefully before getting in too deep. Considering how deep Proster was already into this he was not going to do that. He just looked at the priest and waited for him to continue.

"Proster," the priest's voice as loud enough that Proster almost winced, "Do you swear to keep the people of Proster safe from harm?"

"I do," Proster answered. He tried to speak loud enough that the front could hear him while soft enough that he did not feel it ringing in his head afterward. Fortunately, there were no quivers or cracks when he spoke.

"Do you swear to take care of the people of Proster in all the ways that you can?" the priest said. Proster was sure that it was getting louder with each question.

"I do," Proster answered.

"Do you swear before God that you will rule this kingdom to the best of your ability?" the priest asked. His eyes were now on Proster as if he expected Proster to be struck by lightning if he answered wrong.

"I swear by God and Saint Ingram," Proster answered. The priest looked like he was going dispute that Saint Ingram had anything to do with ruling a kingdom, but he finally signalled for something. Herwin stepped up on the dais with the crown on a red cushion. The priest picked up the crown with both hands. He moved it to just above Proster's head. Herwin stepped back off the dais.

"With God's blessing I crown you King Proster of Proster," the priest said before setting the crown on Proster's head. The thing felt like it weighted a ton and did not help Proster's headache at all. The priest stepped back out of the way. Proster got to his feet and then turned around to face the people that were watching. Once he was turned around and looking out at the people, they broke into applause. Then starting at the front row and going back the people bowed to him. Proster could see the priest had also gone down to one knee.

Proster left them kneeing until he could hear someone mutter something.

"You may rise," Proster announced. People gratefully straightened up.

"I am now officially your king," Proster said, "I battled for this position and I will work hard for things that benefit you."

The crowd broke into applause.

"In the meantime," Proster said, "I want you all to leave."

"What?" the priest asked looking at Proster in surprise.

"By royal decree," Proster said including the priest in his announcement, "Get out." The people in the back had already started for the door. The rest of the group turned as well. The priest stepped down off the dais and glared at Proster before he started toward the door.

"You as well," Proster pointed to Herwin, "Everyone out. I want to be left alone." Herwin headed for the door. Proster herded them out the door of the throne room. Once the last one was outside, Proster closed the doors. He picked up a piece of cloth that had fallen to the floor. He used that to tie the handles together so that no one could open them. Then he went back to the dais. He took the crown off and placed it on the throne. He removed the cape and laid it on the floor. He laid down on one side of it and flipped the other side over himself. Then Proster closed his eyes and let the beating in his head put him to sleep.

Proster took a sip from the goblet in his hand before looking over the crowd. He had slept for several hours before getting up and shedding the awful clothing. It was close to smothering him. He had managed to sneak up to his room for his usual clothes, but on his way back down he had found Herwin and Garrick waiting for him. They had planned a banquet and dance in his honour so that people could celebrate, even if he was not willing. So now, here Proster was sitting at the table set in the court yard of the castle and watching residents danced to the band that was playing.

Proster had noticed two things while sitting here watching the dance. The first was that the band did not seem to know any slow songs. The second being that there were a lot more women at the dance than men. The area for dancing was full of couples, but there were still plenty of women standing around the outside waiting for someone to ask them to dance.

If Herwin or Garrick had stayed, Proster might have asked them if they had planned on there to be a difference in numbers based on what Garrick had said before the coronation. But both had excused themselves for the evening. Proster knew that Garrick had headed for home as soon as the banquet was over, but the disappearance of Herwin made Proster even more suspicious. Maybe Herwin thought that his absence would encourage Proster to be interested in one of the females that were dancing or around the edges.

Proster had looked over the crowd several times with Garrick's words in mind, but as usual not one interested him. It was not like he was completely uninterested in women. He just felt no emotion connection to any of them. There was the slight concern in Proster's mind about not having an heir, but he was still young enough to have several children. And if all else failed he could adopt a boy that he could declare to be his heir. Would not quite be the same as having his own child on the throne, but it was the next best thing.

Proster finished off his drink and shook his head in response to the servant that offered to refill the goblet. Proster set down the goblet and walked to where the party was. He picked the prettiest girl that was standing outside the dancers and asked her to dance. She accepted as if she did not have any other choice. They danced for a song. She was friendly and willing to answer his questions, but distant. When the song was over he bowed to her and looked for another partner.

The girl found him more than he found her. Proster was immediately feeling like he was a meal for this girl and not just a dance partner. Based on what she was saying, he knew she was not interested in him personally, but had an interest in being queen. As soon as the song was over he detached himself and found himself another partner before she could suggest that they dance again.

This woman was nice and willing to talk with him. She did not seem uncomfortable at all. Her fiancé was busy working tonight otherwise she would be dancing with him. Proster enjoyed her company and even suggested a second dance, especially since he saw his last dance partner near the edge of the crowd where they had been heading. The woman was willing and had noticed where his eyes had gone in the crowd. He was able to laugh about it with her.

When this song was through the woman went off with someone else. They had separated on the opposite side of the crowd from the other woman and he had a chance to look around for another partner. A woman from the far side of the crowd caught his attention. She was beautiful. Her brown was long and loose. It fell in waves around her. She wore a green dress that made her stand out in the crowd. She was having a spirited discussion with another woman.

A longing hit Proster like a punch to the gut. It made him want fall to his knees with its suddenness. He was not quite sure what to do. It was as if his mind had become confused about the world around him. Finally, he realized that he had to go talk to her. Yes, Herwin and Garrick would be smug and all the rest of it, but if he could at least met that woman nothing they had to say would matter.

Proster pushed his way around to the spot where the woman had been, but he had lost sight of her in the process. Now she was nowhere in sight even though he was sure that this was where she had been standing. Proster looked around for her. He could not find her. He moved to a place where he could see over the heads of the group, but still could not see her. He wondered if she had been a dream or if she was real. He went back to his seat and took a refill of ale. He kept watching the crowd for the woman, but if she had been there she was gone now.

KING PROSTER IS DEALING WITH BOREDOM AND AGAIN, BUT HE FINDS A VERY UNEXPECTED CURE.

Proster sat on his throne trying not to look as bored as he felt. The guards announced another group of people clamoring for him to solve all their problems. As the people did once a week for the past eight years. There were no new problems or extraordinary problems. Just disputes about property and relationships. It could bore anyone that was forced to sit through them. Proster found that the only excitement that he had managed to drum up during this time was when he got to throw people into the dungeon. He had even thrown some people into the dungeon because they went on so long that he was falling asleep. But even that had lost its excitement. Even the attempts by the people to give him reasons not to throw them into the dungeon were getting boring. And throwing people into the dungeon did not seem to persuade them not to bring their problems to him.

He had actually thought about putting his armour back on and going out with the intent of conquering another kingdom. The last time he had done that it had been exciting for a little while. He could keep going until the continent was his to control. He could have kings in lord like positions and be the king over all the kings. But Garrick had told him that he would be better to stick with what he had. And Garrick had been spending most of his time at the castle since Pepita had died three years ago. Proster had tried to get him to go home and spend time with his children, but Garrick just ignored those comments. With Garrick watching over his shoulder Proster could not take out his armour to see if it still fit without Garrick asking what he was doing.

The thought had occurred to Proster to takeover Grackle. Since his father had died seven years ago his brother Alaric had been running the kingdom. The rumours that had been coming from Grackle since were enough to make anyone wonder if King Thedious had passed his lack of brains on to his on. Alaric was more interested in his family than his kingdom and was trying to be a peaceful man. Grackle had no army since Proster left, aside from the king's person guard, and several kingdoms that Proster had defeated were starting to look to Grackle with the interest. None of Proster's other siblings seemed to have any interest in taking the throne, but there were some power hungry nobles that could see what was coming. Proster had heard a few things from Mati about his father gathering forces. Mati had also said that as a noble of Proster he was going to see what happened without interfering. Proster could use his army and take the kingdom from Alaric. It would not be much of a fight, but it was better that this boredom.

Proster had tried to find things that were exciting and hold his interest, but many times people told him he could not do something because he might get killed. They did not want him to die without leaving instructions on who got the kingdom in case of his death and he had ignored any attempts to discuss that.

Garrick's repeated suggestion was for Proster to get married. Proster pretended not to hear the suggestion on the occasions he did not feel like telling Garrick to shut up or go away. Neither deterred Garrick from offered the suggestion at a different times. He seemed to think that Proster was delaying getting married out of stubbornness. But Proster had yet to meet any woman that he would want to get married to. There were several kingdoms that had sent messengers with portraits and a treaty in marriage. Despite all the ladies being beautiful, he could not see himself waking up next to any of them for the rest of his life.

He had made that comment to Herwin when one arrived. Herwin proceeded to point out that most of the women would expect to have her own rooms. Proster pointed out to Herwin that there were no rooms set aside for that purpose and that had been done for a specific reason.

Proster continued to brood as the people stopped before the dais and bow.

"Rise and explain what the problem is that you bring before me," Proster said. The two men, both looking like farmers, straightened up.

"He stole my cow," the farmer on the left said. He pointed to the farmer on the right.

"He keeps letting his cow eat in my field," the farmer on the right said, "he is taking resources that I need by letting his cow eat them. So I kept his cow when he let it eat my field."

"I never did such a thing," the farmer on the left said, "I was not watching this once and my cow wandered into his field."

Proster could see the fight starting between the two farmers, but he did not bother to say anything or do anything.

The farmers turned to each other to continue to shout at each other. The farmer on the right took a step toward the other one and the one on the left punched him for it. The guards rushed in as it broke into a full brawl. They pulled the farmers apart. The farmers continued to yell at each other, but it was no longer about the cow. They were just yelling insults to each other. Proster had not heard many of the insults before and they were very interesting.

"Silence," Proster's voice boomed. The farmers fell silent, but continued to glare at each other. The guards let them go and both farmers bowed to Proster.

"You," Proster pointed to the farmer on the left, "With will pay him the amount equal to what your cow ate. You," Proster point to the farmer on the right, "will give back his cow."

The farmers bowed again.

"And you will both pay a fine of twenty silvers," Proster told them before they could turn to go, "for wasting my time."

The farmers did not look happy as they bowed for a third time, but this time they left the throne room.

"You did not just throw them into the dungeon for fighting in the throne room?" Herwin's voice came from behind Proster.

"Some of their insults were amusing," Proster said as he signalled for the guards to turn anyone else that wanted an audience with him away.

"There is rumour going through the streets," Herwin said, "That the wizard is still alive and has turned you into a golem."

"I thought you would be at home with your wife," Proster said as he stood up.

"She told me that if I needed to be a mother hen that I should come back here," Herwin said, "And then she ordered me out of the room. I have requested a messenger to bring any news to me."

"Between you and Garrick I can hardly do anything without being given unnecessary advice," Proster said. He stepped down off the dais and headed toward the door to his study.

"That is our jobs," Herwin said.

"Then you need to take a vacation," Proster said, "so that I can get a break from both of you."

"Or you take some of our suggestions," Herwin said as he followed Poster into the study.

"Because your suggestions have very little to do with how I choose to run this kingdom," Proster said, "and more to do what you believe is behaviour not befitting a king. I did not conquer a country just to become my father."

"You succeed in that," Herwin said.

"Then quit pushing me to become him!" Proster turned to Herwin and said the last part into his face before turning back around. He head for his desk.

"I hardly think," Herwin started.

"You have not thought about it at all," Proster said, "I did not want to become a king that reins from a throne with no connection to the people. That was part of why I did not want to have a coronation. Now that I suffered through that the people are bowing and want me to be above them all. I remember my father doing that. In fact I remember a time where he demanded to ride through the market place rather walk because he did not want to get that close to the peasants. That is not what I consider to be a wise ruler."

"And yet you do not even blink at the idea of being a golem for an evil wizard," Herwin said.

"I consider most of that something to do with idea in you and Garrick's heads about how a king is supposed to act," Proster said, "and perhaps a little bit of boredom."

"If you were any more bored you would be out of your chair and into the brawl that just took place in your throne room."

"And have to deal with the lectures from you and Garrick?" Proster asked, "Why would I subject myself to that on purpose?" Proster started going through the papers on his desk.

"And how would you change things if Garrick and I were not pushing you to rule this way?" Herwin asked.

"I think I have run out ink," Proster said starting to look through the drawers of the desk.

"I will have some more brought," Herwin turned toward the door that led to the corridor.

"Do not bother," Proster said, "Lamont told me that he would have to order some the next time I ran out. I know which shop he purchases the ink form. Perhaps a walk would do me more good than arguing with you."

"You still have not answered my question," Herwin said.

"To start with I would not have a set time a day for people to bring their petty complaints to me," Proster said as he headed for the door to the corridor. Herwin followed him out of the study.

"Is that to prevent them from seeing you at all?" Herwin asked.

"No, that would be so that they could bring me things any time," Proster answered, "Right now they line up outside and hope that they get a change to come in. If they arrive late for some reason they do not get to see me even if what they are bringing is urgent."

"That still does not change them bringing their petty complaints," Herwin said.

"The changes in my head would filter out those too," Proster said, "It is as easy as having someone who the people can go to and negotiate their troubles without bringing them to me. Then I can deal with the important stuff." They passed the door out of the castle.

"Should we have not turned there?" Herwin asked pointing to the corridor they just passed.

"No," Proster said, "I have no intention of going out into the market place wearing this." Proster gestured to the fancy outfit that Garrick and Herwin had convinced him to wear for days that he saw the people.

"Even if they realize who I am before they rob me, I would still get people coming up to me and bowing,"

Proster said, "I would rather get through the market place without any bowing."

"So, you would rather have someone else listen to the people's petty complaints," Herwin said, "Which sounds a lot like someone else doing your job for you."

"What I was thinking was someone who could deal with problems like the one I just dealt with," Proster said, "ones, where they just need someone to negotiate between them. Someone else to say cut the cow in half and you each get part of it."

"You did not tell them to cut the cow in half," Herwin said.

"Great," Proster slapped Herwin on the back, "I am so glad you are willing to take the job. That takes a load off my back."

"I did not say that," Herwin said.

"I even have a room set up just for you and dealing with people," Proster continued as if Herwin had not said anything, "There will be two guards assigned to help you. You will need them if anything gets out of hand. I will have Fulton ask people their business when they arrive at the castle door. Depending on their answer they will be directed to me or you. You can deal with the minor squabbles and I can deal with anything big. I will have to make sure that Fulton can tell the difference."

"What if I cannot be here?" Herwin asked.

"Garrick can take over for you," Proster answered, "It solves so many problems."

"Like how to get your advisors out of the throne room while you make decisions," Herwin said.

"If it is important I ask your advice," Proster said, "If there is anything that I need your advice for I will make sure that you have your chance to comment on it as well as Garrick. Half my problem right now is that you two have been hovering over me giving advice on matters that I do not need it and it is not always the best advice. It comes out as how you perceive I should act as a king and not how I can make this kingdom better. I have been making decisions all my life that had affected other people and not all of them have been bad ones."

"You are not thinking of attacking another country, are you?" Herwin asked.

"Before I do so, I will ask for your advice," Proster answered as they stopped at his bedroom door, "I did the last time." Proster went into his room and closed the room behind him.

He came out five minutes later. This time he was wearing shirt, trouser and cloak. All were in darker colours and looked worn. He would not stand out in the market place. Herwin was still standing there.

"You have done this before," Herwin said looking at the outfit.

"I cannot stay in the castle all the time," Proster said, "That would just make things worse than they already are."

"Any other changes that you feel are necessary?" Herwin asked as they started back down to the first floor.

"The increasingly bothersome question about marriage should be eliminated from both you and Garrick's advice," Proster answered.

"I do not believe that is likely to happen until you accept the idea and actually get married," Herwin said.

"I am not choosing to remain unmarried," Proster said, "I have not found a woman that I want to marry."

"And how do you intend on finding a woman you want to marry?" Herwin asked. They left the castle through a side door and started across the court yard. None of the guards paid any attention to them.

"Unescorted visits to the market place help," Proster said, "Not being trapped in the castle by my advisors are another way. Be given time and space to make such decisions on my own."

"We are just worried about the kingdom," Herwin said, "Especially since you have gotten bored."

"If I told you that you had to leave Misa and marry someone else, would you do it?" Proster asked.

"No," Herwin answered as they left the castle gates and headed towards the market place.

"Then why are you demanding that I just pick one woman that I do not love out of the crowd and marry her just because you think I should?" Proster asked, "That is not going to cure my boredom and it will just prove to me that taking your advice is not good for me."

"And what about your kingdom?" Herwin said.

"I really do not care," Proster answered, "Once I am dead, the kingdom is not my problem. I am in good health and the only people around me that have even thought about my death are my pesky advisors. I will get married when I find the right woman. The future of the kingdom can be dealt with from there."

Herwin did not say anything as they reached the market place and Proster directed them towards a shop, but Proster could feel his disapproval, it radiated like heat off a fire. Proster ignored it as he usually did. It was not his fault that Herwin and Garrick could not see reason on the whole issue of marriage. It was not like Proster had not explained it to them multiple times or tried different arguments. He really was not worried about the kingdom after his death. His legacy was in conquering the kingdom, not in making sure that there was an heir to the throne.

Proster strode purposefully across the market place with Herwin trailing behind him. The shop where he would buy the ink was on the other side of the market place from where he and Herwin entered. Proster had bought ink from there before. As usual Proster was watching the crowds that he walked passed. He liked to see what normal people were up to and doing with their day. Not to mention it meant that he noticed pickpockets and thieves before they got close to him. Proster's gaze fell on one woman that was talking to a cooper outside his shop.

The woman had long brown hair that fell down her back in a braid. She wore a dark green dress that showed off her curves. The material was of a good quality without being expensive. The woman and the cooper looked to be discussing the barrel that was sitting on the street between them. It looked like they were talking about some defect the barrel had and she was not interested in the barrel with a defect. Her hand gestures and body animation suggested a spirit that Proster had not seen in a woman in a long time.

Despite it being a clear and sunny day Proster felt like he had just been the centre of a lightning strike. There was this sudden urge that bubbled up from inside him to run over to the woman and take her into his arms. Sweep her off her feet and take her back to the castle. Anything to have her with him. The rest of the world faded away and the woman seemed to be the only thing left in it. And the only thing in the world worth having. It was like she was the only thing in the world for him and he did not mind it.

Slowly the rest of the world came into focus. Or at least enough that he saw no ring on her finger or husband at her side. He guessed her to be doing some business for her father.

Proster stumbled a little when he realized that he had started to slow down. He stopped himself from falling and once again focused on his destination, though the image of the woman seemed to be imprinted on his eyes.

"Are you okay?" Herwin asked.

"I am fine," Proster answered, "I just tripped over my own feet."

Proster went to the shop he wanted and Herwin followed him inside.

"Good morning," the shop keeper greeted them, "What can I do for you today?"

"I need ink," Proster answered, "One bottle now and the rest shipped to the castle in the next few days."

"Yes, Lamont had put in an order," the shop keeper said, "He said that someone would be by when it was needed." The shop keeper took out a bottle of ink and set it on the counter.

"Five silver," the shop keeper said. Proster took out his pouch and counted out five silvers. He handed them to the shop keeper.

"Here you are," Proster said. The shop keeper took them and offered the bottle of ink to Proster.

"Here you are," the shop keeper said, "And have a good day."

"You too," Proster said as he took the bottle of ink. He put it into his pouch before putting the pouch away. Then he left the shop with Herwin following him. Proster looked toward the cooper's shop and saw that the woman was gone. He looked over the market place, but she was nowhere in sight. Proster continued back through the market place. He did not see the woman again. Once out of the market place Proster and Herwin headed back up to the castle.

"How often do you go and buy ink?" Herwin asked.

"About once every six months," Proster answered, "I go to the market for other things as well. It is a great excuse to leave the castle. I am surprised that you had not noticed before."

"Apparently I was not paying attention," Herwin said.

"And how did you figure that I was successful at not going crazy?" Proster asked.

"It is a fairly large castle," Herwin answered, "And you have been known to spend time beating up on practice dummies in the court yard."

"I was raised in a castle," Proster said, "it gets boring really fast. The beating up on a practice dummy is more to keep me from getting fat with all the fancy foods that the cooks keep making. If I did not doing something I would not be able to fit on my throne let alone do anything else."

"You can ask the cooks to make something else," Herwin said.

"I have asked the cooks to make other things," Proster replied, "It is like talking to you and Garrick about my marriage. No one hears what I say, even though I am the king of this country. Apparently I can be king of a country without being king of myself."

"Have Lamont talk to the cooks," Herwin suggested.

"Because obviously I have not thought of that before," Proster said, "like any foolish person I would not bother try getting my message across other ways."

"Okay," Herwin said, "There should be some way to get the cooks to stop."

"I was thinking of firing them all and replacing them with people who would listen to me," Proster said, "but Lamont said that it would be difficult to find any more cooks. After I asked how easy it would be to find another castle steward he said he would see what he can do."

"You are going to fire all the cooks?" Herwin asked.

"I would fire my advisors to see if that would help with the marriage problem as well, but I already made them lords," Proster said, "which makes it harder. And I would have to figure out to get new advisors that I thought I could trust, because with advisors you cannot just hire any person off the street."

"Have you told the cooks that you would replace them if they did not listen?" Herwin asked.

"How could I ever do that?" Proster asked, "They might think that I was serious about having them change the way they cook. And then they might not be as deaf as my advisor, who has not yet heard anything I have said all *morning*."

Herwin did not respond. He seemed to be thinking up other ways that Proster could get the cooks to change without firing them.

Proster sped up as they walked back to the castle. He was just short of running and could feel his heart speeding. Herwin was still trying to keep up with him and was quickly out of breath. Proster thought about speeding up some more, but decided that Herwin already could not talk.

They reached the castle sooner, but Proster did not start slowing down until they were just about to the door into the castle. Herwin continued to follow him inside, but was waylaid by Lamont before they got very far inside. Proster went to his study by himself. He left the bottle of ink on the desk before leaving the study again. He went up to the second floor and into the library. The walls in the library were floor to ceiling with shelves, except the wall that was toward the court yard of the castle which was all windows. These windows made sure that a person could sit in the library all day and not have to light a lamp. It also meant that a person could stand at the windows and watch everything was happening in the court yard. Ignoring all the chairs and the table with a pile of books that he had wanted to read, Proster went straight to the windows. He took off his cloak and threw it behind him onto the chair that was there.

His mind was no longer on Herwin, the cooks, or the work he needed to get done. His mind was back on the woman from the market place. Her image was still in his mind as if he had seen her less than a minute ago. He still wanted to find her and hold her close. His palms itched to undo the braid and run his fingers through her hair. He wanted to hold her to him and never let her go. Without even knowing anything about her, Proster felt like he was addicted to her presence.

Proster wondered if you could fall in love with someone after have seen them briefly just once. He had heard about such a thing from fables. The prince would fall in love with the maiden from a glance at a hundred metres. But that hardly seemed possible in the real world. Love required getting to know the person and finding that they were a good match. It required time see all sides of the person. Did it not?

A memory came to Proster. It was of a woman who was standing across a dance floor from him. She too had long brown hair and wore a green dress. He compared the memories, but could not tell if they were the same lady or not. He had not gotten a clear look at the one from the party and seemed more like a dream than a memory. It had also been a long time ago. Had that been his coronation? Or another party that his advisors had him go to? Proster could not remember anymore, but he definitely remembered the woman from the market.

Proster set his forehead against the glass as if hoping to cool it off and stop the heated thoughts that were running through it. He looked down into the court yard. There was the woman from the market place. She was riding beside a man sitting in the driver's seat of a wagon that had barrels in the back. They were pulling up to the door in the court yard that was used to take goods to the store rooms.

Proster blinked. The woman was still there. He rubbed his eyes. The woman had not disappeared from where she was sitting beside the man. She was not an illusion created by his mind just because he was thinking of her. She was real and she was in the court yard.

The man sitting beside her looked similar to her. They shared the same skin tone and basic facial structure. His hair was no longer brown, but silver. He also appeared to have one leg that was misshapen. The wagon stopped just passed where Proster knew the door was. The woman got down off the wagon and went to the door. The man stayed in the driver's seat. She must have knocked before a moment later two of the cook's helper came out. They started to unload the barrels and take them into the castle.

Proster heard the door to the library open, but did not turn around. He eyes were still on the woman below in the court yard. The one that seemed to have the ability to make his heart beat faster just by existing.

"Lunch is served in the dining hall," Lamont's voice came from the doorway.

"Where are Herwin and Garrick?" Proster asked.

"Herwin is busy setting up the room you said to give him to be negotiator," Lamont answered, "Garrick received a message that he was needed at home. He left after Herwin assured him that you would not be left to your own devices."

Proster was quiet for a moment as he hesitated to ask the question that was on the top of his mind. Lamont stayed where he was and waited.

"Who is the man delivering barrels?" Proster asked. Lamont came into the room and to the window next to where Proster was standing.

"That is Baback and his daughter Ruana," Lamont answered, "He is the wine merchant that we buy most of our wine through."

"Have them both come see me in the throne room when they are done," Proster said, "I would like to speak with them."

"Yes, sir," Lamont said, "Will there be anything else?"

"How are you doing with your search for new cooks?" Proster asked.

"I have found one replacement," Lamont answered, "But no others."

"Replace the one that talked to me that last time that I asked to talk to the cooks," Proster said, "Perhaps if he is replaced then the rest will do things the way I want them to be done."

"Yes, sir," Lamont said. He turned and headed out of the library.

Now that I asked to speak with them, what do I say? Proster wondered. It is not like I can just ask him to give me his daughter. And if I were her I would have some problems with someone asking for me. She is not just some serving girl that I want to keep me warm for one night.

Proster shook his head as he turned from the window. He forced himself to start towards the door. He wanted to turn back and continue to watch the woman, but knew that he was going to have to go to the throne room if that was where they were going to be sent.

Another memory came into Proster's head. A memory of an old man. Proster had met the man one of the first few times he had snuck out of the palace and roamed the streets. The man had been sitting by the fountain in the centre square and feeding the birds pieces of bread. Proster had been curious about the man, but the other boys that he had found to play with just told him that the man was sad and then moved on to other things. That day the other boys were not around so Proster had gone to the man. The man started telling Proster about his life. He sat there because he had no need to work, but no one at home to keep him company since his wife had died.

The man talked briefly about other things, but came back to his wife. He had said that he had met his wife one day in the market place. He had come to the market place to talk to a merchant about the quality of meat his servants had been getting from that merchant. He had just finished and was leaving the shop when he saw a woman across the market place. She was begging for food from someone passing by. He had been struck with how beautiful she was. The man said that he had fall in love with her at that first sight. He claimed that God must have pointed him to the one woman that he was supposed to marry. He had gone over to the woman and offered her some money for food. She had smiled at him. He had immediately dropped down to his knees and asked her to marry him. He figured that something inside her was saying the same thing that he was hearing because she said yes. After that he thought he could not live without her. But she had died and he had continued to live. And he missed her more than anything in this world.

Proster was not sure that God had anything to do with what he was feeling right now, but given that he had not given Saint Ingram his due in a while Proster was not sure that anyone up there was willing to listen to him or watching out for him. Still the feelings were real enough as far as he could tell. So after spending all morning arguing with Herwin about not wanting to get married he had now seen the one woman in the world he wanted to marry. He could not even say that he had met her. It was only seen and he was not sure that she would feel the same way.

Was he ready to ask for her to marry him based on not knowing her at all? Was he ready for that leap? What was the point of asking to speak with them if that was not his intention? Why did he not going down to the court yard and talk with them? That would a lot less embarrassing than having them come to the throne room and have him stutter through his feelings, which are based on nothing but seeing her in the market place. Could he explain that without looking completely stupid and idiotic? Would they understand or would they think he was a flake? No one really thought that love at first sight was possible, did they? He did not and he was suffering from it. All the diseases in the world and he had to suffer from love at first sight. Why could he not get something that was easy to deal with like leprosy? At least then people would leave him alone.

Proster reached his throne room. No one else was there as he walked across the room to the dais. He sat down on the throne and looked around the room.

Back when he had taken over the kingdom the throne room was bare. Now there were decorations of red, white and gold. He had wanted blue and gold, but someone said that red, white and gold were the colours in the crown. After that everyone said that red, white and gold were the colours that throne room should be. Proster suggested a new crown. He was beginning to resent the people around him but those people were the ones that he had gathered and knew that he could trust. He was going to have to figure out how to get people to listen to him. That was his problem. No one listened to him or took him seriously. The cooks or his advisors.

Ruana's lips looked so kissable when Proster had seen her through the window. It added to the want to wrap his arms around her and never let her go.

Would she and her father take him seriously? Would they listen to what he had to say? Would they just think that he had gone crazy? He felt like he had gone crazy. Proster was sure that someone came to him and said that they had fallen in love with him from a distance that he would have thought that they were crazy. Love at first sight is an insane idea, but if it was not possible why would they have a name for it.

Proster started picking at a loose thread on his trouser. He realized that the thread was brown. It dawned on him that he had not changed clothes since he had gotten back from the market place. He was still wearing the clothes that he wore to the market place. Now he was sitting on throne looking for like a peasant and nervous enough to being waiting for his execution. That would not make a good impression. Yet going all the way back up to his room would mean that Proster would not be there when they arrived to speak with him, which would not look good either. Proster remembered the shirt had had left in his study. It was still relative clean and looked a lot nicer and he could just slip in there and switch shirts and still be here when they arrive.

Proster was just about to get to his feet when the door to the throne room opened and a guard stepped inside. Proster sent a prayer to Saint Ingram for the right words to say to Ruana and her father to get what he wanted.

"Baback, the wine merchant and daughter," the guard announced. Proster relaxed back into his chair a little bit.

"Send them in," Proster responded. The guard opened the door the rest of the way before stepping to one side. Ruana helped her father as they entered the throne room. Her father's leg was a lot shorter than it should have been and there was definitely a loss of muscle, but he had a presence that suggested he was not a man to walk over or mess with. The crutch he walked with could have easily been a weapon as a walking stick. Ruana had the same type of presence. She was not going to let anyone stand in the way of what she wanted, nor would she let people walk all over her because she was a woman.

She glanced up at Proster as she and her father came towards the throne. Her hazel eyes gave off similar feelings to what Proster was feeling himself, either that or he was deluding himself. Proster stood up and stepped down off the dais.

"How about we sit over here," Proster signalled to the table which was much closer to them. He headed for the table. Ruana looked at her father to see if this was something he was willing to do. He shrugged and turned toward the table. He did not know what the king wanted, but he was not going to refuse the offer of a chair, especially since the king do not seem to be offering out of pity. If it had been pity Baback would not have accepted. Proster pulled out the two chairs to make sure that they were ready before pulling out and sitting down in the next one. The fourth chair had been removed for something and had not been brought back. Which did not bother Proster, because if necessary he would just pull the throne over to the table.

Baback sat down in the chair across from Proster. Only once her father was seated did Ruana sit down.

"We brought all the wine that you paid for," Baback said, "Since we brought what you paid for. That means we both have what we want from the deal and you did not ask us in here to talk about that. Added in that it would be Lamont that would discuss that with us."

"The wine is not why I wanted to talk to you two," Proster said.

"What is it that you wish to speak to us about?" Baback asked.

"I would like your permission to ask your daughter for her hand in marriage," Proster answered.

Baback looked thoughtful and glanced at his daughter. She looked back at him. There was a mixture of emotions on her face. She looked torn between confusion and longing. Proster guessed that she had seen him at some point and was feeling the same thing he was, but she was not sure what it was or had not had the time to examine her feelings. Baback nodded to himself.

"You have my permission to ask my daughter for her hand in marriage," Baback said. He spoke as if he knew exactly what was happening between Ruana and Proster. Proster nodded. He stood up and moved to beside Ruana's chair before getting down on one knee. Holding out a ring with an emerald in it that he had removed from his left hand earlier.

"Ruana, will you marry me?" Proster asked.

"I do not even know you," Ruana answered.

"I know," Proster said, "But something is happening between us that I do not understand. But I know that if you accept my proposal we will have the rest of our lives to figure it out."

Ruana thought about that. Proster did not move as he waited. Time dragged on as she thought about things.

A sound by the door made them all look at direction. It sounded like Herwin. But the guard turned him away. Proster looked back at Ruana and Ruana looked back at him. Their eyes met and the whole rest of the world disappeared. As far as Proster could tell the world revolved around those hazel eyes, brown hair, and lightly bronzed skin.

"Yes, Proster, I will marry you," Ruana whispered. Proster slipped the ring on to her hand. He kissed her hand

"I have to go check on some things," Baback said, "You two get to know each other." He got up and left the throne room. Proster got up off his knee as Ruana stood up. For second it looked like she was going to follow her father, but he left the throne room. She turned back to Proster. Ruana stepped away from the table and towards Proster. She held out her hand to him and he took it. He pulled her to him and she came willingly. Proster wrapped his arms around Ruana and pressed her lips to his lips.

Proster sat in his study looking at the pile of paper work that he needed to get done. He had been keeping up with the paperwork until today. He spent most of the day with Ruana and avoiding Herwin. So far he had been successful at avoiding Herwin, but he did not think that would last. However, Ruana and her father had headed for home. She would come back tomorrow so that they could plan their wedding. Proster had already given Lamont a list of requirements. Now Proster had to deal with the pile of paperwork before tomorrow or have to face a bigger pile.

There was a knock on the door to the corridor.

"Yes?" Proster called as he picked up the first paper to read. The door opened and Herwin stepped inside. He closed the door behind him.

"Where have you been?" Herwin asked, "Every time I asked someone they directed me to a place that you were not at."

"I have been having trouble sitting still today," Proster answered, "And you were busy with other things."

"It is set up," Herwin said.

"Good," Proster said, "Then you can start tomorrow."

"I heard Lamont say that you will busy tomorrow," Herwin said, "What is going on?"

"Nothing important," Proster answered.

"Does it have something to do with Lamont running away with a long to do list?" Herwin asked.

"A little bit," Proster answered.

"And it is nothing I need to know about?" Herwin asked.

"You will find out as soon as you need to know," Proster answered.

"So, what are you hiding?" Herwin asked.

"If I tell you then I would not be hiding it anymore," Proster said, "And then you would not be trying to figure out what it is. But it has nothing to do with you."

"I heard that you fired one of the cooks," Herwin said.

"I told Lamont to fire one of the cooks and replace him," Proster replied, "All in an effort to get the rest to listen to me. Tomorrow I will find out if it worked."

"There are better ways of doing that," Herwin said.

"Good, then you go take over your own kingdom," Proster said, "Then you can come back and tell me how to get people to listen to you. Because in my kingdom, no one listens to me."

"You are king, everyone listens to you," Herwin said.

"Wonderful!" Proster said, "Get out. I have work to do."

"Why are you hiding something from me?" Herwin asked.

"Because I am tired of you not listening," Proster answered, "Out!"

"I-" Herwin started.

"Out!" Poster go to his feet and shouted. Herwin looked taken back for a moment and then he left the study. He closed the door behind him.

Proster started into the pile of paperwork.

A week passed with Proster and Ruana planning their wedding. Proster started ignoring Herwin and Garrick when he could not find them something else to do. They did not seem to understand what the problem was. The cooks stared serving meals that fit with what Proster told them.

The wedding was set up on the balcony of the castle so that as many people as could fit into the court yard could see it. The priest that conducted Herwin and Garrick's weddings offered his services, but Ruana turned him down before Proster could say anything. Ruana found a priest of Saint Ingram to conduct the ceremony, even though it would be a more traditional ceremony.

On the day of the ceremony Proster put on his dress uniform in the guest room as his room was being redecorated. Herwin and Garrick had to deal with guests. Lamont had to deal with anything else that had to do with the ceremony. He knew that Ruana was getting ready in a room down the corridor from him. She was there with her new servant and her father. He was going to walk his daughter from the room to the alter so that he could give her away. Proster had found him help at the winery so that Ruana would not be as worried about her father.

Proster left his room and went to the balcony where he was supposed to be. The priest was already there. Proster nodded to him as he took his place.

"I trust that you have asked Saint Ingram's blessing in this matter," the priest said.

"I did," Proster replied.

"Good," the priest said, "From things I assume that the bride is not a worshipper of Saint Ingram."

"That is correct," Proster said.

"That is why I have not brought up payment," the priest said.

"I have heard what your usual fee is," Proster said, "I arranged for you to collect it from Lamont at the end of the ceremony. I do not expect you stay beyond that."

"Thank you very much," the priest said.

"It is heavier than usual as I doubled the amount from your usual fee," Proster said, "for having to perform a traditional ceremony."

"May you be blessed with fortune and good luck," the priest gave Proster a slight bow.

The wedding march started playing. Ruana and Baback came through the door in time to the music. It was not far until Baback handed Ruana to Proster and moved back to the proper distance. Ruana's dress was white lace. The lace was double in places to make it proper for public viewing, but Proster could see a lot of skin in the places where it was not double. She had skipped the veil and just wore the tiara that Proster had found for her. She wore the matching necklace, earrings, and bracelet. As far as Proster was concerned she was the beautiful thing in the whole world. The priest started into the sermon that was written for such an occasion.

Proster looked into Ruana's hazel eyes. Happiness filled his heart and echoed back in those eyes. For the first time in a very long time he felt complete. He had found the place he was supposed to be and with the only woman he wanted to love. The world felt right. Perhaps that was why he had been bored, he was looking for the other half that would fill in his time.

"Proster," Priest turned to him and handed him the wedding band. Proster nodded.

"Ruana, I take you to be my lawfully wedded life," Proster said, "Before these witnesses I vow to love you and care for you as long as we both shall live. I take you, with all your faults and strengths, as I offer myself to you with all my faults and strengths. I will help you when you need help, and turn to you when I need help. I choose you as the person with whom I will spend my life." Proster slipped the wedding band on to Ruana's finger.

"Ruana," the priest said handing Ruana the other wedding band.

"I, Ruana, take you, Proster, to be my husband. To share the good times and hard times side by side. I humbly give you my hand and my heart as sanctuary of warmth and peace, and pledge my faith and love to you. Just as the circle is without end, my love for you is eternal. Just as it is made of incorruptible substance, my commitment to you will never fail. With this ring, I thee wed." Ruana slipped the wedding band on to Proster's finger.

"I declare you to be married," the priest said, "Kiss your bride."

Proster drew Ruana to him and he kissed her. She kissed him back.

CONCLUSION?

Mitchell closed the book and set it down on the table beside him. He picked up his glass of brandy and stared into the fire. His father had died less than a week ago. He left Mitchell several boxes of books that were old. Mitchel had never seen books quite like that. Although based on things his father had never read them, just received them from his father and stored them away. Mitchell had opened the box and taken out the top one. It was in very good condition for its age. This Saturday had been the first time that Mitchell had time to read that top one. There was still several more in the box.

The books were strange. They were made up of leather and parchment. The writing was handwritten with ink that did not look like a pen. There were no dates in the book that he had read. Yet they talked about a country of Proster, which was around still today. Mitchell was sure that one of his ancestors was a writer and these were just his manuscripts. Nothing like this could have taken place in real life. Mitchell had studied history in school and on his own after that. There was nothing like this in any of the history books.

Mitchell took a sip of brandy and the thoughts swirled around in his head. The clock on the mantle chimed. It was only two o'clock. Mitchell got up and went to get the next book out of the box.

ABOUT THE AUTHOR

Heather Mantler is a lover of fairy tales and fables. She is also a student of psychology. She lives in Prince George, British Columbia. Heather is always working on another story.
Heather encourages all her readers to post their reviews on Amazon.com